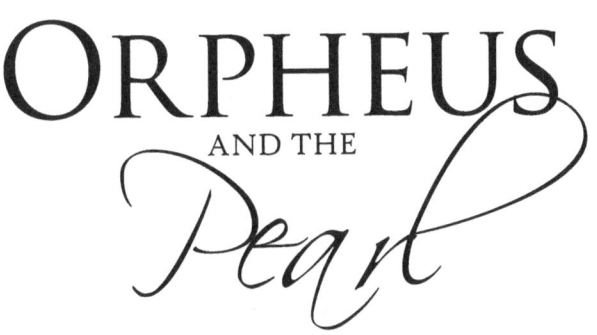

ORPHEUS
AND THE
Pearl

KIM PAFFENROTH

—◆—

OR
THE FEAST OF FLESH

DAVID DUNWOODY

ORPHEUS AND THE PEARL

Kim Paffenroth

NEVERMORE, OR THE FEAST OF FLESH
David Dunwoody

2nd Edition 2018
1st Edition Trade Paperback 2010

All Rights Reserved

Dark Recesses Press
657 Craigen Road
Newburgh, Ontario
Canada K0K 2S0

Cover art by Jodi Lee
Edited by Jodi Lee

ISBN: 978-1-988837-15-4

TABLE OF CONTENTS

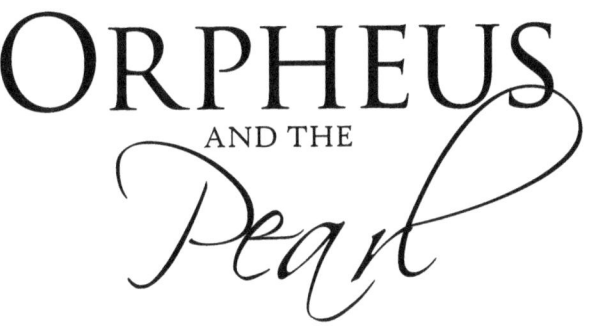

KIM PAFFENROTH

ACKNOWLEDGMENTS

Extensive, detailed comments on and critiques of this story were generously offered by Dr. Marylu Hill. She did so as I progressed in the writing, so I could work on many of the details of the time period. Dr. Dan Morehead, a practicing psychiatrist, offered comments on the clinical aspects of treatment. The story is much more accurate and believable as a result of their work, for which I can't be thankful enough. Dr. Robert Kennedy looked over the final product and offered his insights and encouragement, as he has on many of my previous works. Louise Bohmer gave the manuscript a thorough copy edit, as well as promoting it constantly and enthusiastically since then, for which she has all my appreciation and thanks.

For those who are interested in the background of this story and how it relates to my other job as a professor of religious studies, I think you will notice that there is much less overtly Christian influence in this story than in my other works. As I have looked back on it, I have been surprised that it is in fact my most overtly Platonist piece of writing, though I think elements of the climax go beyond that worldview, and may even overturn and undermine it. (I still await the trenchant final analysis of Dr. Philip Cary on this issue.) But, now I'm talking like a professor or a pedant: real beauty overcomes such distinctions and such rationalizations, and I hope you find something beautiful in these pages.

Kim Paffenroth
Cornwall on Hudson, NY
April 2009

ORPHEUS AND THE PEARL

Catherine stepped off the train onto the platform of the Worcester station after an uneventful ride from Boston. She had been instructed that someone would meet her there, and immediately a large, severe-looking man approached her. He was a towering bulk dressed in a plain black suit that could not have been comfortable on such a warm, spring day. Catherine noticed from under the brim of her hat that his face appeared to have but one impassive expression, for it registered neither interest nor surprise at seeing her, neither friendliness nor hostility as he strode up to her. Catherine tried to estimate his age relative to her own thirty-four years, but his rugged, immobile features were of such a kind that he could have been the same age as she or much older.

"Dr. MacGuire," he said slowly and distinctly in a voice that was as free of intent or emotion as his face. There was not even the slight rise at the end that would indicate the usual interrogative tone in such a greeting; it was as though he were rather telling her name, or saying it for no reason at all.

"Mr. Romwald?" She had been given the name and description of the man who would be picking her up at the station just the day before.

Romwald almost imperceptibly nodded and deftly picked up her two large bags. She followed him to the doctor's automobile, a common sort of conveyance in Boston for some time, but only appearing in significant numbers this far out in the country after the Great War.

On the bumpy ride to the doctor's large estate, Catherine again reflected back on the odd events that had brought her here, and wondered what further surprises were in store. Two days before, out of nowhere, a young assistant had called her away from some rather pointless research numbers, to speak with her research director. The senior professor explained that he had just spoken on the telephone with the very famous Dr. Wallston. All her director could say was that she was to go to the doctor's estate outside Worcester, but offered no further details of what she was to do there or how long she would stay. While it certainly gladdened her immensely to get away from the deadly dull research that was forced on her by senior faculty who lacked imagination, creativity, or even competency, the whole thing smacked of melodrama and intrigue.

Catherine forcefully expelled her breath to blow some stray red locks from in front of her nose, and sourly reflected that both melodrama and intrigue almost inevitably meant that yet another of the old lechers, with whom she was forced to work, was going to try clumsily and disgustingly to get under all those folds of cloth around her middle and see if the carpet matched the curtains. That was how one of them had so crudely put it to her during a pawing session from which she had barely managed to extricate herself, an escape that probably had doomed her to many more years of research drudgery rather than her own appointment and work.

But, she had to admit, all her cynicism and bitter disappointments notwithstanding, Dr. Wallston was not the typical faculty, even if he had some reputation as a Lothario. Not only did he lack nothing in competence, he was one of the most brilliant men of his age. His work on the nervous systems of both primates and humans was nothing short of revolutionary, and there had been steady talk of a Nobel throughout the second decade of the new century. But last year he had suddenly left public life to retreat to his estate and care for his ailing wife, who had subsequently died. There were then constant rumors that he would soon return to his brilliant work, but so far, he had remained in seclusion in this western redoubt, whose gates the car was now passing through, bouncing along between rows of the most enormous sycamores Catherine had ever seen. Past these, the road wound through rolling fields, around the side of a large hill, and then approached the main house, which sat atop a lower hill, overlooking a lake. Except for the automobile, they could have been in the American or European countryside in the previous century, or even the one before. Raised in the city, Catherine was enthralled by the bucolic setting, and silently cursed herself for all the beautiful spring days she had spent sterilely sequestered in laboratories and libraries.

Romwald ushered her out of the automobile and into the large and elegant home. He didn't offer her anything in the way of rest or refreshment, instead moving directly to the door of the doctor's study, while she stood in the foyer and quickly straightened herself somewhat. He opened the study door, and Catherine stepped into the room as confidently and professionally as she could. The door closed behind her noiselessly.

Dr. Wallston had already stood and was now coming around his desk to greet her. He was still a relatively young man, tall and impressive, with a full mane of black, wavy hair, grey only around the temples. The rumors of his many trysts seemed much more believable now in person.

"Dr. MacGuire, thank you so much for coming, and on such short notice," he said as he shook her hand.

"Dr. Wallston, I was honored to receive your invitation, of course." She was glad and put somewhat more at ease by his use of her title. She could expect it of a servant like Romwald, naturally, but physicians much further down the pecking order than Dr. Wallston had seen fit to call her "Miss" MacGuire, or worse, by her first name. She could feel her jaw clench, even now, when she thought of how some had even resorted to "Cathy" or "Kitty," usually with a leer, as though she were some pretty, little Irish whore in Scollay Square, instead of the educated expert she had sacrificed so much of her life to become.

"Please, sit." He returned to his chair behind his desk, folded his hands and sighed. "Dr. MacGuire, I need your help in a most grave matter, a matter that has confounded me now for several months. You come highly recommended, and I believe that in this matter especially, your unique perspective as a woman may also be of crucial importance to its successful resolution."

"Dr. Wallston, I'm flattered at your confidence, and grateful that my director saw fit to recommend me for such a difficult assignment." The last part was a shameless lie. Her director was a total incompetent who seldom hid his disdain for her, but enjoyed gawking at her enough to keep her around. Even better, he had so far restrained any further attentions to only occasionally touching her bosom or buttocks—even having what he must've considered the 'decency' to make these tactile intrusions seem accidental—so Catherine tolerated her servitude with him. Catherine didn't let even the tiniest muscle on her face betray her untruth to Dr. Wallston, nor give away the sudden, wrenching twist in her stomach at the mention of how her gender might be important.

She knew all too well how important it was to men that she was physically different than they, even if she were their intellectual equal or superior in every way. "But I really can't imagine what medical problem I could assist with, if it escapes your knowledge and skill." This statement, on the other hand, was completely true; sometimes toadying was also sincere, and this made it a hundred times less demeaning.

He looked at her steadily, his head slightly tilted down. Unlike most men his age, he did not wear eyeglasses, and Catherine had to catch herself and blink, to break her reverie on how beautiful were his hazel eyes – so full, not just of intellect, but of emotion. And right now, that emotion was one of an oppressive sadness and resignation. "No, you flatter *me*, Dr. MacGuire. It is true that I have much knowledge of many physical afflictions and how to cure or treat them, more knowledge than most any man of our age, more knowledge than any man has ever before had. Perhaps, I fear, more knowledge than any man should have." He sighed again. "What a strange thought. Do you think that possible... to have too much knowledge of how to cure our afflictions?"

Catherine sat, unblinking, for a moment. The question was as odd and unexpected as this whole errand. "We are doctors. We have taken an oath to do good and never harm to our patients."

"Quite so. My point exactly. What if there are afflictions that are for our own good?"

Catherine craned her neck forward. She sincerely hoped the conversation did not get any odder. Though many would call her choice of profession the height of impracticality, she was, at her core, an imminently commonsensical and anchored person, not given to such metaphysical flights as the doctor now seemed to be proposing. "I don't think that is for us to judge, doctor. If most people in our society deem something a mental or physical evil, then we must do everything to alleviate it."

He nodded and frowned slightly. "Yes, I was afraid you would say that. Afraid, because it is by following that line of reasoning that I have reached this current impasse. I alleviated what most people agree is a very great affliction, perhaps the greatest evil of all, only to find that the cure brought a host of other pains and sorrows. And that is why I have called you, for these new forms of pain are not purely physical, and therefore they are far outside my expertise."

"They are of a mental nature then, doctor?"

"Yes, though I believe you sell your expertise short, doctor. I asked you to come here because you have studied psychology, especially psychoanalysis and the new theories and practices of Dr. Freud, theories with which I am unfamiliar, for illnesses far different than I am prepared to cure or even acknowledge. I can repair most any injury to the nerves or the brain, and therefore, so far as we know, most any damage to the *mind*. A stroke, paralysis, memory loss, epilepsy, seizures – I've cured all of them, even the most severe cases, with surgery and drugs. No, Dr. MacGuire, I fear the problems I now face are matters of the *soul*, and your science claims, after all, to heal the soul. Unless you think that too extravagant a claim? Do you not believe in the soul?"

The conversation had now gone from being odder than Catherine had imagined it might be, all the way to being odder than Catherine *could* imagine a conversation being. "I'm afraid I don't understand, doctor. If you have a patient who requires psychoanalysis, I will do everything I can to help that person. I am quite sure, however, that matters of religion or belief have no place in this discussion or in the treatment of disease."

Dr. Wallston smiled ever so slightly at her, those beautiful, sad eyes still fixed on hers, and she felt the tickling on the back of her neck that one gets at such approval and interest when they are welcomed and mutual. "Well, there was a time when I surely would've agreed with you on religion's irrelevance, but now I am not so sure." He paused, then slid a sheaf of papers across the desk toward her and handed her a Waterman pen. "Regardless of religion's relevance, however, I am afraid that the relevance of the merely human law is beyond debate or discussion. This is your contract for your services here. I think you will find it generous, and, despite the necessary legal language, fairly straightforward."

Catherine picked up the papers and skimmed them as quickly as she could. As the doctor had said, it was fairly straightforward, in that the stipulations were few and clearly stated. The content of those stipulations, however, surprised her. The main point seemed to be that she was never, under pain of law, to divulge or discuss what she saw or did at the estate. She didn't know what to make of this, but she didn't know how to ask about it, either. And the far greater surprise was the matter of payment. She looked up at the doctor from behind the papers. "Doctor, there must be some mistake with the contracted payment. Perhaps a simple matter of an extra zero?"

He smiled a little more broadly at her. "No, Dr. MacGuire. If you can, in fact, help me with this patient, then that will be a small enough sum, weighed against the nearly priceless benefit you will have brought to me." After she signed, he took back the papers and stood. "It is, however, late in the afternoon, and I have several other things to which I must attend. Romwald will show you to your room in the west wing and bring you dinner later. Please feel free to go about the grounds in front of the house, but I must ask you not to enter the gardens behind the house, nor the main building, until tomorrow morning after nine o'clock." He walked over to the door and opened it for her. "Thank you again for coming, Dr. MacGuire."

Romwald wordlessly showed her to the west wing of the house, which was separated from the main building by a breezeway. The separate wing consisted of two small bedrooms, a bathroom, and a sitting room. All the rooms were open and her bags were in the sitting room, as though she were free to choose either or both of the bedrooms for her stay. The arrangement soothed her somewhat frayed nerves after the odd interview, for it would make the living arrangements much less awkward and scandalous, as she would have a good deal of privacy. And if she were going to practice psychoanalysis on someone, she would probably be here for quite some time. Despite most people's imagination that one simply lay down and talked about one's mother for a few minutes, then walked out a new person, the reality was a much longer, messier, and more ambiguous process. She wondered if even Dr. Wallston, as knowledgeable as he was, knew how much it would entail.

After settling her possessions into one of the bedrooms, Catherine walked out through the breezeway. Taking two steps towards the back of the house, she saw Romwald walking out from the back of the house into the garden, carrying a tray with tea service, so she retreated toward the front of the house, as per the doctor's warning. She went back down the drive to the bottom of the hill then followed a small stream there, through sycamores somewhat smaller than those at the gate. She sat under one of them and enjoyed the freedom and beauty of this strange, almost otherworldly place into which she had so suddenly and unexpectedly landed.

A while later she made her way back to the house and found dinner waiting for her in the sitting room. Since Romwald was the only servant she had seen or even heard mentioned at the estate, she supposed he had prepared it as well as brought it, and she judged him an exceptional cook. The fish chowder, pork chops with rosemary, and glazed carrots were some of the most savory things Catherine had tasted in ages, though living alone was not conducive to doing much in the way of creative cooking, and she certainly didn't have the money to dine out. She thought it rather rude to leave the tray and dishes there in the sitting room, but again she heeded the doctor's warning not to enter the main building. After some ablutions in the bathroom she changed into nightclothes.

Returning to the sitting room, she saw that the tray and dishes had disappeared, another example of Romwald's stealth. She went back to the hall and tried the outside door, but found it locked. She had half-expected it to be so, given the general tenor of her visit so far. Well, if the building caught on fire during the night, she could always go out the window, she supposed, so there seemed no real harm. But she still felt rather like a prisoner, even if she now knew that she would be one of the most handsomely paid prisoners of all time.

Catherine was exhausted, but too restless to sleep, so she drew all the curtains and settled herself in the sitting room, reading one of the books there. The selection in this room was somewhat unexpected in a medical doctor's home, as it seemed to be all literature. She picked a copy of *Jane Eyre*, a story she remembered loving as a girl. After a while, when it must've been quite late, she heard voices in the main house, then a door opening. She heard scratching on the outside door to the west wing, and what sounded like the doctor's voice saying, "No, dear, not there, no. Come away to bed. You're tired. We'll talk about it tomorrow." The scratching continued, then there was some unidentifiable growling, and finally Catherine jumped and sat bolt upright at the sound of a very high, loud, and sustained shriek. There was the sound of scuffling, more growling, and the door to the main house slamming shut. Then Catherine was left sitting there for several minutes that seemed so very much longer – eyes wide, heart pounding, breathing through her nose in short and silent huffs, her fingers gripping the arms of the chair as tightly as she could, until she darted to her bedroom and locked the door.

After those nocturnal events, Catherine quite understandably did not sleep well, but she roused herself early, dressed, and went to the sitting room where breakfast had appeared as surreptitiously as dinner had. She ate, then puttered about the room until the little clock on the mantle there finally chimed nine o'clock. At that point, she dared to try the outside door, which was now unlocked. She found the door to the main building similarly unfastened, and she entered. Not having been instructed where to go at nine, she went to the only room she knew, the doctor's study, and knocked on the door.

It was almost immediately opened, and there again was Dr. Wallston. "Good morning, Dr. MacGuire," he said as he stepped aside and motioned for her to enter the study. "I hope you are rested and ready to begin your work this morning."

Catherine felt enough toadying had been done yesterday, and she needed to know a bit more of the goings on here if she were ever to survive and not go mad from lack of sleep, never mind be able to conduct her treatment effectively. "My nighttime rest did suffer from some unusual noises, doctor."

He frowned slightly. "Yes, I'm sorry about that. I had certainly hoped you were asleep by then. It was, as I'm sure you guessed, the patient. Sleep is perhaps the most difficult of her daily routines, for the medicines she is taking leave her exhausted, but also agitated, so she is both too tired, yet unable to fall asleep. But she is resting and recuperating physically right now and we will see her shortly."

Catherine nodded, but also frowned. At least she knew the patient's gender, but she would need much more information. And how could the doctor have a female patient here alone in his home? Perhaps she was a relative, an unfortunate sister or niece.

"Doctor, I'm sure you know enough of psychoanalysis to understand that I must have a great deal of the patient's history and the exact nature of the disorder before I can even begin to proceed. I will need that before I see her this morning."

"Of course, yes, I understand. I'm afraid, however, that it is quite complicated, to say the least, for she suffers both physical and mental disorders. Much of her condition will have to be shown to you, in order for you to appreciate it fully, rather than simply explained. But I know that I must do everything I can to give you the information you require, as difficult as it may be for me." He still had not sat, nor offered her a seat, which seemed strange, but the stress of explaining the situation seemed to be distracting him from the basics of propriety or even simple practicality, so there they stood as he continued to describe the situation. "I am sure you know that my wife died late last year. Christmas Day, to be exact."

"Yes, doctor, I had heard. Everyone in the medical community was greatly saddened by your loss."

"She was much younger than I, even a little younger than you, so it just wasn't fair. I took it upon myself to right that injustice, Dr.

MacGuire. What no one outside of this house knows is that I was able to revive her that Christmas Day."

Catherine tried to fit the statement into the accepted categories of medical phenomena and physical laws of biology. "Revived? You mean, she was only unconscious and she awakened? Or was she briefly in a coma?"

Dr. Wallston shook his head very slowly and again did not take his eyes off her, nor she off him. "No, definitely not a coma. All respiration and heartbeat had stopped. Physical death by any definition we know."

Catherine could feel her eyes widening, but she was still trying to understand what the doctor was saying or implying, and she was still not willing or able to step beyond the boundaries of logic or reason. She blinked and tried to will her eyes into a calm and controlled expression, even as she felt them not cooperating. "Then I don't understand what you're saying, doctor."

"That's why I had so much trouble broaching this with you. When my wife fell ill, I greatly accelerated the experiments I had been performing on stimulation of the brain and nervous system. I barely slept for months, not just proceeding along the paths I had already charted, but constantly trying new methods, elixirs, or chemical compounds, even those from unorthodox sources. Chinese and African folk medicine, leaves chewed by South American warriors before going into battle that supposedly give them superhuman strength and bravery, reports of trance-like states induced in people in the Caribbean or in charismatic Christian sects, even speculations about the volcanic gases that might have seeped up into the Temple at Delphi to 'inspire' the oracle there. I investigated practically any heightened mental state that had ever been reported, to see if I could reproduce any part of it. I, of course, did not want just the sleep or stupor that so many plants and drugs induce. If I were to find something that might help my wife, then I needed to know what causes the frenzy, the ecstasy, the whirling dervish, the rapid-fire glossolalia, all the phenomena where people seem to go outside themselves and beyond their normal consciousness, not just sink down into it, as in sleep or death."

He paused to shake his head again. "But of course, my experiments on animals showed me how little the body could tolerate such extreme forces. Our little garden is the graveyard for hundreds of animal corpses that have broken backs, burst blood vessels, compound fractures from their mad convulsions, paws bitten off as they ravaged themselves, faces torn off by their own frenzied claws. When my poor Victoria finally died of fever, I had developed a chemical compound so potent and yet so precisely calibrated to her size and weight that I thought it might be able to excite and stimulate the nervous system even of a corpse… without, I prayed, destroying the subject in the process. Once she passed, I had to work very fast, of course, before there was brain damage, but she had already been packed in ice to try to quell the raging fever. It gave me the time I needed to administer the elixir. And, in short, it worked. My Victoria awoke, stood up, walked, and spoke. She was back with us. I was overjoyed." There was a faint smile at the recollection of a moment that must have been the happiest and proudest of his life.

Catherine still did not quite believe what she was hearing, but at least it had been presented to her in terms that skirted close to the logical and possible. "But, why would you keep this secret? If this is what happened, then this is the greatest medical breakthrough in all of human history."

His smile vanished as he shook his head again, slower and more sadly than ever, and she felt a lump in her own throat, seeing his beautiful eyes glistening with tears. "Oh, I certainly thought so, at first. Even before I had properly rejoiced with Victoria myself, I was thinking of when I could get to town to send the telegram, informing the world of my *Great Deed*. The Nobel Prize? There would be no prize commensurate to the very conquest of death itself!" His frown was more of a sneer now and he nearly spat the words out. "Fool! Proud, vain fool! There is no prize for being the maddest fool that ever lived. So intent on how I *could* cheat death, I never stopped to think of whether I *should*, of whether such a thing would be good, or damnable. No, doctor, I soon saw that one does not advertise, let alone brag, when one violates the most basic – I dare say, the most sacred – laws of nature. For beginning soon after she awakened, Victoria has been overwhelmed by an all-consuming rage which I do not understand, which she will not explain and cannot control, and which Romwald and I struggle to contain, lest she hurt herself or someone else. I have conquered her body's death, only to make all of us prisoners to her mind's torment. This is why I have sought out your help."

"Dr. Wallston, I don't know what to say to such an account." But Catherine's practicality again asserted itself, despite the unbelievability of the doctor's story. For ultimately, it made little difference what Mrs. Wallston's exceptional, even unique physical journey had been. Today she was a patient whose pain Catherine might be able to diminish, and immediately that settled all other matters. "I will do whatever I can to treat Mrs. Wallston and improve her condition. Please know that I will do whatever is necessary, whatever is possible, and whatever is within my power and knowledge." She knew it was terribly forward, even scandalous, but she couldn't help putting her right hand on his arm, lightly. "If there is anything in modern science that can cure her pain and yours, I will find it." And despite her skeptical statements of the previous day, she felt it necessary to add, "God willing."

He let her hand stay where it was for just a moment, before stepping back slightly and letting Catherine withdraw her hand. "Yes, I believe you will agree how necessary God's will is in this matter, when you see the severity of the problem." He walked to a large, dark wooden dresser and opened the top drawer. "Please come over here, Dr. MacGuire." She stood next to him and saw that in the drawer was a leather jerkin of some kind, together with large, thick gloves of the same material, and a metal helmet, much like the soldiers had worn in the Great War, though with the sides bent down more, so that they would come closer to the wearer's collar, covering more of the ears and neck. "She's so violent that I must ask you to wear these, at least when you first meet her. Romwald wore them at first, but she's gotten used to him and me. It's mostly changes in the routine now that send her into a murderous frenzy. She becomes so savage that she may even try to bite you, and you must be especially on guard against that, for the wound might be so septic as to be fatal." He held up the jerkin. "I wouldn't want you hurt."

"Oh, do you want me to take that back to my room and put it on?" She didn't quite understand what he was suggesting.

Dr. Wallston saw her confusion, and blushed now at his own lack of perception. "Oh, no, it fastens in the back, there's no way you could put it on yourself." At this Catherine was blushing much more than he, though his own redness deepened several shades beyond hers when he realized what she thought he was suggesting. "Oh, but it's very large, as we made it for Romwald, so you need only take off your jacket, nothing more."

Catherine cleared her throat and took a deep breath. Having a man watch her unbutton her jacket seemed much more lewd than the simple fact of being in front of him in only her blouse, so she turned her back to the doctor as she unfastened the buttons, removed her jacket, and draped it over a chair. She turned back towards him and he held up the leather jerkin so she could put her arms in it. She then had to turn away from him so he could fasten it. There was a pause. "Dr. MacGuire, I'm sorry, I hadn't reckoned on all the details of having a woman wear this. May I ask you to let down your hair? It won't fit under the helmet otherwise, I'm sure."

The blood was rushing back to her face again. "Well, at least fasten the jacket and then I'll take care of my hair."

There was another pause. "That would be another problem. I think it best if the hair went under the jacket. Again, changes and surprises seem to incite my wife to a particular fury, and I am afraid the site of your long, red hair would be much like the red capes bullfighters use."

Catherine knew her hair incited enough negative attention in men, she hardly doubted that it could have a similarly deleterious effect on a deranged woman. But it was still galling, as though she flaunted it or brought it on herself. What was she supposed to do? She was already three-quarters of the way to being a eunuch; she bitterly thought how she might as well shave her head and finish the job. She half turned back toward Dr. Wallston, her eyes narrowed, her teeth clenched, and her voice just a whisper. "What are you implying, doctor?"

He was stammering and as flustered as she. "Nothing. Please, doctor, I just think concealing your hair would be more therapeutic at this time."

"I see." Catherine turned away from him again. As with the buttons, to let down her hair while facing him would be more whorish than anything she could imagine or endure. She reached up and pulled out the pins and let her hair fall. Dr. Wallston took the rather enormous flow of curls and laid it on her back, then gathered in the strays locks and gently smoothed down the soft and vibrant mass with his hands. Catherine very deliberately kept herself from stiffening or flinching at his very nearly inappropriate touch, but really, she felt little inclined to bristle, for his touch was neither suggestive, nor was it as awkward and tense as their verbal exchange had just been. Instead, she could immediately feel how he had successfully earned his reputation as a seducer, for his touch was purely and simply comfortable, confident, and natural.

Equally comfortable was how he finished, letting her hair alone before it became impossible to ignore the inappropriateness of their position, leaving her with a calm and pleasant memory instead of more embarrassment. She could feel him fastening the lowermost hook, then working his way up, tucking her hair in at each hook. When he was finished, she turned and he offered her the gloves and the helmet. She put these on. There was a mirror above the chest and she saw herself, how absurd she looked, like some Medieval pageboy at a battle or tourney. All she needed was a halberd or lance to complete the picture.

Dr. Wallston checked his pocket watch. "Let us go prepare to see the patient, doctor. It's nearly time."

Dr. Wallston led Catherine into a hallway near the back of the house where there was a pale blue curtain suspended on the wall. The curtain did not reach the floor, but only hung down about halfway. Dr. Wallston pulled the curtain aside, revealing a window behind it, about a foot high and six feet wide, set at eye level. This window looked into an immaculate, tiled room, almost blinding in its total and extreme whiteness, for not only were the tiles this color, but so was every other item in the room. On the left side of the room was a door – or rather, an oval metal hatch with a circular handle and round window in it, the kind of watertight hatch they would have on board a ship, or on the new, hellish weapon of war, the submarine. Catherine looked to the left and saw that there was a door a few feet down the hall, and she suspected the hatch and that door both connected to an anteroom to allow access to the tiled laboratory. In the middle of the tiled room was an enormous tub, standing about four feet high and also made of white tiles. It was filled with a liquid which, if it were not for the stark and complete whiteness of its surroundings, might have also looked pure white, but which the contrast revealed to have a touch of yellow in it, like cream or buttermilk. The surface rippled and swirled slightly, as though there were currents or motion under the surface, and very faint wisps of a yellowish steam or fog drifted up from it. There was a metal grate in the ceiling above the tub, into which the yellow vapor drifted. Also in the room were a large table and cabinet by the wall, a smaller table with towels on it by the tub, and a folding screen near the back.

Dr. Wallston pointed at the metal hatch, the tub, then up at the grate. "We have to be extremely careful with the revivification elixir and the vapors from it. It is a compound of the most potent nerve stimulants, and it would be highly toxic to any person who was not already dead. A whiff of the vapors would induce tremors and mild hallucinations. Any contact with the liquid would bring on vomiting, convulsions, and death almost immediately."

"And for Mrs. Wallston what is the effect, or the side effects?"

"Motor and mental stimulation to normal levels of activity. I've also added emollients to keep her skin and hair from drying out. But of course, with such stimulants, we can't administer very much at once, or the effect would be fatal, similar to how it would affect a person not already dead, so she must bathe in it daily. She ingests a tiny bit as well, to keep her digestive organs stimulated and working. As I said, nighttime is when we see the primary adverse side-effect, the difficulty in sleeping, for by then the stimulation is wearing off to the point where she cannot move about normally, but she cannot fully relax and sleep. As you know, of course, our bodies do not require sleep, but rather, our brains do, or we would go completely mad, so it is crucial that she sleep, rather than simply give her more stimulants to keep her awake constantly. She has the chemical bath in the morning, so she can function normally through the day. I do not know if the chemicals have any part in her maniacal rages. I have repeatedly and meticulously gone over all the constituents and their properties and effects, and there is no clear connection. I fear it is some aberration or disorder much more deeply ingrained in her mind, in her soul." He shook his head.

Catherine nodded and watched the room, expecting Mrs. Wallston to emerge from behind the screen and enter the tub. Instead, two small hands slithered from out of the cream-colored liquid and grasped the sides of the tub. At first, they were hard to see, as they were so pale that they were indistinguishable from the stark white of the sides of the tub. Even the nails were the same shade, like chalk. Catherine gasped and her gloved hand instinctively covered her mouth. She was later quite amazed that she had stifled a scream, but really, the situation seemed beyond such a reaction. It was, quite literally, breathtaking. Following the hands, a head of wet blonde curls emerged. Under the curls was a pair of large, dark goggles, like a welder would wear; the black of the goggles and their strap was the only contrast in the room, since the blonde hair was so light, almost platinum. A woman's upper torso slowly and gracefully rose beneath the head, her breasts just breaking the creamy liquid's surface. Most hideous of all perhaps, neither her lips nor her nipples had the slightest tinge of pink. The woman stood, turned away from them, and stepped out of the tub. Her entire body was all the same ghastly hue. It was not emaciated, as Catherine might have expected, but really rather fulsome and curvaceous. The figure from the tub took up a towel from the small table and wrapped herself in it as Dr. Wallston closed the curtain.

"It will take her a few minutes to dry and dress herself. Are you all right? I know this is difficult, but you must be prepared for the more unusual and disconcerting aspects of my wife's condition."

"Yes, I know, I'll do my best. But Dr. Wallston, we were standing here for several minutes. How did she stay submerged for so long? I have to understand what's going on if I am to compose myself."

"My wife no longer breathes, Dr. MacGuire. She is completely submerged in the chemical bath for two hours each morning."

Catherine blinked, trying to take this in. "But you said you *revived* her, doctor. I don't understand what her condition is, if she is revived but doesn't breathe."

"I know that term was a little misleading, and I apologize for that, but there is no sufficient or accurate term in our language. I had thought to call the process 'reanimation,' but that too is misleading, for she is not simply moving about mindlessly like a puppet or an automaton. She has all her faculties of speech, reason, thought, and emotion. She is active, deliberate, mentally aware, and therefore, I believe, fully human and alive, even if she lacks some of the incidental, physical qualities of what we label 'life.'"

As in their previous conversation, Dr. Wallston's explanation had come closer to putting his wife's condition into normal, understandable human categories of thought and analysis, but it was still far wide, to say the least. "'Some physical qualities,' doctor? I dare say most of us consider breathing a little more than 'incidental' to life, wouldn't you? I don't know how to comprehend or deal with what you are presenting to me."

"I know, doctor, I know, and I apologize again. But there is nothing I can do at this point. My wife is now what she is, and I hope you will still strive to treat her."

Catherine pursed her lips. "You know I will. It is my duty and, I hope you realize, an all-consuming passion to which I have devoted my life."

"Yes, and I hope you know how grateful I am."

She paused, then pursued her investigation to understand, as calmly and clinically as she could. "Circulation?"

He shook his head. "No. None."

"If there's no circulation, how do the chemicals get through her system?"

"Partly, the chemicals' effects are carried along the nerves, the way pain or any other information is carried through the nervous system. Also, it is why she has to soak for such a long time, to let the chemicals penetrate the tissues adequately. That's another reason the chemicals are so dangerous to handle: the molecules are so rarefied they penetrate most anything."

Catherine felt her stomach briefly convulse. She did her best to keep down the bile and hide any sign of her discomfort. A walking corpse was unnerving enough, but the idea that the poor woman was pickled daily was somehow much more nauseating. After a brief pause, she asked, "Body temperature?"

"Exactly equal to her surrounding environment. We have had to keep the house quite warm in the winter months, lest the cool temperature inhibit her functions, the way it would any cold-blooded animal. I am very much looking forward to the spring and summer to alleviate this. She was always so vibrant and lively in the summer months."

"Digestion?" She remembered thinking how perfectly shaped Mrs. Wallston's body still was, even in her unnatural state. Other than the pallor, she looked like the beautiful, well-fed, pampered young woman that she had been in life.

"Oh, my, yes. That is another of her urges I don't fully understand. Victoria is consumed with an overwhelming hunger, and for the most *robust* fare. Since she doesn't metabolize like we do, I knew her needs would not be nearly as much as a grown adult, but I had anticipated that she would need a small amount of nutrition in order to sustain her bodily motion and to repair damaged tissue, so I had thought to feed her simple foods, as you would a small child. Cooked vegetables and breads and cereals. These meals caused some of the first violent outbursts from her, and since then she has demanded nothing but barely-cooked steaks and room temperature scotch."

"Scotch? Is that a wise addition? What are its effects on her?"

"None. Without circulation, it never reaches her brain, or liver, so there's no danger of any of the usual damage from alcohol. There are not even any signs of intoxication. She says she just likes the taste, but I suspect it's more recalcitrance, as though she enjoys the sheer naughtiness of drinking something so unladylike, as strange as that may seem." Catherine didn't think this sounded the least bit strange, unlike everything else she had heard. "It's the steak that's the real problem. We try to keep the quantities as small as possible, but the nearly raw meat is hard for her to digest, since she lacks all bodily fluids, such as stomach acids. We have partly solved this with gullet stones."

This time Catherine couldn't keep the retching down to the pit of her stomach, and she audibly gagged. Again, it was one thing to have to get over the unnaturalness or hideousness of the situation. But the indignities to which the poor woman was constantly subjected made her gag instinctively and sympathetically. "Gullet stones?"

Dr. Wallston had lapsed into the enjoyment of clinical details and analysis that often make doctors go on about things that should demand respect or tact, and not fascination or excitement. "Yes, as in birds. Surely you know…"

Catherine could not help her glare, nor her rising tone. "I know what gullet stones are, Dr. Wallston! I'm not some neophyte who chats with people on the couch, who practices the 'talking cure,' because I couldn't master anatomy or biology! I was expressing surprise that you fed your wife rocks, for God's sake! It's as though you've turned her into some lower order of creature so she could continue her savage, bestial feasts. And all of this brought on by her being made into some unnatural monstrosity, through no choice of her own, I might add." She paused and calmed slightly. "I'm sorry, I'm not judging you. It's just some of the details are particularly horrible and difficult to accept. I will do my best to look at them dispassionately and help her."

He hung his head. "Again, I know. You have to understand, once she was revived, there was nothing I could do but think of ways to continue her existence. I couldn't very well just stop administering the chemicals and let her die again. It would be like murder. And I couldn't stand to lose her again."

They both heard the clank of Mrs. Wallston opening the hatch. Dr. Wallston went to stand next to the door through which she would next pass. It opened, and she stepped into the hall. "Victoria," Dr. Wallston said, meekly. "I told you someone would be arriving to help with your treatment. This is Dr. MacGuire. She comes highly recommended."

Mrs. Wallston was wearing a long white dress. It billowed out hugely from her small frame, both in the skirts and in the gauzy sleeves. Her hair was neatly put up. In life it surely would've accented her fine features and fair complexion with an enormous shock of shining, glowing yellow, but in death everything was nearly the same exhausted shade, like an overexposed photograph in which one can barely make out the details or contours. And her eyes. They had clearly been a stunning pale blue, but without moisture they could neither glisten, nor shine, nor flash, so they were as dull as if they were made of unglazed porcelain. They had the same fair hue and matte finish as a robin's egg. Catherine could not stop gazing into them, their soulless beauty was so mesmerizing.

Mrs. Wallston tilted her head down and cocked an eyebrow. There was the same growl as Catherine had heard the previous night, before the laryngeal resonance resolved itself into human speech. "Recommended, Percy? Recommended for what, pray tell? With a name like that, and young as she is, I can't imagine it's for anything other than a maid, and I don't need a maid, as you well know." Mrs. Wallston smiled, but with gums the color of lard and no joy behind the expression, it was not very becoming. "Although decked out like that, do you have something else in mind? Stable boy? Perhaps you're taking up falconry or jousting, Percy?"

Catherine knew she had instantly flushed way past crimson at the insults, but there was no avoiding it. Dr. Wallston tried to overlook his wife's monstrous rudeness. "I need the help of another doctor, Victoria."

"And you couldn't bear to have one of your male colleagues see what you've done to me, Percy? Couldn't bear to have them see my freakish body, or my ruined mind? And what? I'm supposed to bare my soul to this tarted-up bit of fluff?"

It seemed to Catherine that she felt Mrs. Wallston slam into her before she saw her move or heard her shriek. But she must've seen her, for she had instinctively raised her right arm to protect herself. The nails of Mrs. Wallston's right hand raked Catherine's cheek, as her other arm grabbed Catherine's, and those hideously beautiful eyes, narrowed now in rage, lunged toward her. Catherine barely kept from falling as Mrs. Wallston, oblivious to either decency or pain, clamped her jaws down on the forearm Catherine had raised in defense. Her teeth were no danger through the leather, but Catherine wondered at the force of her bite; it seemed much more powerful than what the human jaw muscles should be able to exert. Dr. Wallston had grabbed his wife from behind and was shouting for her to stop, but for several seconds all three of them were struggling, before he got her off and put himself between the two women. He had a hold of his wife's shoulder as he looked to Catherine. "You're hurt. Are you all right?"

Catherine could only nod, tasting the blood as it trickled down to her mouth from the four gashes on her cheek. She was panting for breath after the unexpected assault, and she could see that Mrs. Wallston stood impassively, not breathing at all, and with a grotesque attempt at a smile curling her lips. Dr. Wallston still tried to take control of the situation. "Victoria, will you please stop?! This is serious."

Mrs. Wallston wrenched her shoulder free of his grip and took a step back. "What's serious, Percy, is how hungry I am. The same gnawing hunger you've condemned me to every minute of this purgatory. With all your foolishness about bringing an Irish nurse-maid into the house, at least I can count on long-suffering Romwald to fix a decent steak." She shrugged. "Have your esteemed colleague join us, if you must." She fixed her hellish gaze again on Catherine. "I don't care about your cold comfort or pity, *doctor*, so long as I get some steak and scotch that are both warm. I feel a little chilly."

Catherine had removed her Medieval garb and stanched the bleeding of her cheek, but foregone a bandage. The deepest gash, from Mrs. Wallston's middle finger, might leave a scar, but the other three were barely noticeable even now.

Mrs. Wallston was at the far end of the table, the sunlight from the window behind her throwing her front into shadow. Dr. Wallston was at the middle of the table and rose when Catherine entered. The seat closest to the door was empty, and Romwald appeared from the door to the kitchen and pulled it out for her. In front of her and Dr. Wallston were bowls of a potato and onion soup. As discreetly as possible, so as not to incite another incident, Catherine glanced at Mrs. Wallston's plate and saw four paper thin slices of steak. Even from this distance across the table, the shiny redness of both the meat itself and the blood that pooled on the plate were vivid and nauseating to Catherine. Next to the bloody plate was a water tumbler of scotch, the amber liquid swirling with the oily currents of strong liquor.

Mrs. Wallston fell to her carnivorous repast with gusto, while Catherine and Dr. Wallston sipped more daintily at their soup. Mrs. Wallston made little attempt at conforming to typical table manners, smacking as she chewed and slurping the scotch. Catherine could swear she heard the clacking of the rocks inside the dead woman, and once again she had to exert herself to keep her stomach from heaving. When Mrs. Wallston belched loudly, they ignored it, but the second time Dr. Wallston tried to intervene, however mildly. "Victoria, please, we have a guest."

Mrs. Wallston looked up from her plate for the first time. Now her lips were obscenely painted a glistening crimson from the bleeding meat. She took up the scotch for a long gulp, which at least had the benefit of mostly clearing the blood from around her mouth. "What, Percy?" Mrs. Wallston sneered. "She's Irish, for God's sake. You know how they are. I'm sure she's heard and seen worse around the dinner table, haven't you, missy? Your dear old mum probably had quite a brood running about, since you all breed like vermin. And doubtless father was always in his cups, hmm? Pshaw. My dainty little burp shouldn't faze her a bit."

Catherine looked up and dabbed her mouth with her napkin. The woman's snipes about her nationality were much more painful than probably even Mrs. Wallston could have guessed. Catherine's grandparents had given up their religion and changed the first letters of their last name when they came to this country, to try to pass as Scots and Protestants and give their children a chance at a better life. When Catherine had learned that her name was the English or American version of her grandmother's name, Cathleen, it had hardly seemed to her that the name was honoring the family, but just another badge advertising their shame, like the all-too-conspicuous mane that she had to carry with her everywhere. And to what had all these various sacrifices and subterfuges amounted? For Catherine, a head full of knowledge and skills she wasn't allowed to use, years of abuse and scorn from men, and now even this unnatural hag, this thing that shouldn't even exist, could cruelly taunt her with impunity and a perverted glee. It was all she could do to keep from bolting from the room. But as ashamed as she was, years of practice and emotional calluses kept her nailed to her chair with her face completely expressionless.

Dr. Wallston put his hands on the table. "Victoria, please! She's right there! And she's come to help! Please! I can't do this alone anymore." His voice was cracking. He clearly hadn't slept well in months, and he was at his wits' end now with the infernal situation he had himself created.

Mrs. Wallston clearly reveled in her ability to shock and hurt everyone around her. "Oh, poor Percy, embarrassed that your little Irish tramp is more ladylike than your wife? I'm sure she's a good deal warmer, too, but what difference is that to me? I'll tear her throat out with my teeth as soon as you're out of the room, dear, and then she'll get right down to room temperature, I'll warrant."

There was a moment of silence. Then Catherine again fastened her burning, green eyes onto Mrs. Wallston. When she spoke, her tone was as icy and even as the stare of Mrs. Wallston's two frozen orbs. "I assume you two were raised not to use the third person when speaking of someone who is present, unless that person is a servant or a child. And let us be quite clear, I am not the servant or inferior of anyone here."

"I'm sorry, I never said you were," muttered Dr. Wallston.

"If you wish to remain the loathsome, little beast that you are playing at the moment, Mrs. Wallston, then I will gladly get on the next train back to Boston. If it's threats you enjoy, then let's have a good and proper row right here and get it over with. But if you want me to stay, so that perhaps you and your husband can return to something resembling a normal, or even a happy existence, then you will address me by my title. And you *will* apologize."

Catherine had no idea where the words had come from, or what their effect would be. She had actually been formulating something quite different when those words had come tumbling out instead. And even if the part about fighting Mrs. Wallston was mostly adrenalin induced bravado, it had felt like the right way to address the situation.

Mrs. Wallston took another drink of scotch, sipping it tidily, and kept her eyes fixed on Catherine. "Please believe me, doctor, when I say that no one is more sorry for the way I am than I, myself. You have now been forthright with me, and that is something that deserves much better treatment than I have given you. I am sorry I was rude to you. Will that do?"

"Yes, it will do quite well, thank you."

"Good. Would you like some scotch? It's really quite exceptional, and I expect, with your anatomy, you might enjoy it even more than I do."

"Yes, thank you. That would be nice."

After lunch the two women retired to the sitting room in the west wing. There was a couch there on which Mrs. Wallston sat, while Catherine sat in the same large chair she had the night before. Dr. Wallston was surprised she was already willing to sit alone with Mrs. Wallston, but there was no other way to conduct therapy. Besides, Catherine thought with grim humor, to be the first doctor to die at the hands of the first reanimated corpse was a sort of scientific milestone of which she could be proud, even if it had not been the one she had had in mind all these years.

Mrs. Wallston kept her humor as well, even if her demeanor had softened. "So, do I start talking about my parents now?"

"No, it's not like people think. We don't just come out and force you to talk about certain things."

"Oh, all right. Don't you take notes?"

"No, it's distracting to both of us. I'll write everything down when we're finished."

"So what do we talk about?"

"Well, what do you like to do?"

"I like to read. These are all my books. Many are from my father's house, he is a professor of literature at Brown University."

"I noticed they were all books of literature and not medicine. I wondered what the doctor was doing with such a collection."

"Oh my, he considers literature quite frivolous, I think. That's why they all ended up out here and not in the main building. But there is so much in these pages. So much beauty that I sometimes wonder how they came to be in such an ugly world. And what about you, doctor? Do you think literature a frivolity, too, like my husband?"

"No, not at all. I once thought to study literature, but there were even fewer women studying it than were in medicine, so I found myself gravitating towards that field."

"Well, I never thought to study it at school. I hardly think my parents would have approved of such a course. School was something a nice young lady did in order to be interesting and attractive to a man, not to pursue beauty and knowledge for their own sakes. And then when I got married, I hardly had any time to read. It's one of the few advantages to being dead, having all this time to read."

"Why didn't you have time before?"

"Oh, I was always doing so much work around the house. Romwald is a most helpful and efficient man, but I liked to do as much as possible myself. I suppose it was a habit from when I grew up. My mother always made me do so much of the work around the house. I just became used to it and expected to do it when I had my own home."

Catherine nodded impassively, not wanting to let on that Mrs. Wallston had already talked about both her parents. "So, you haven't had other servants besides Romwald? I thought perhaps Dr. Wallston had kept only him on after your... illness, but I assumed there were others in the house before."

"No, only Romwald. He always did the heavier, manual work, as in repairing the buildings, shoveling snow, raking leaves. And, of course, the driving. But I did all the cooking and cleaning, and most all the gardening."

"I see." It seemed a strange arrangement for an extremely wealthy woman, but now was not the time to investigate. "And what sorts of books have you read since... this year? I was reading *Jane Eyre* last night."

"Oh yes, any novel I can. I know it's silly, but I hope you don't find it too funny that I read Mary Shelley's monster story as soon as I was cognizant again of my surroundings. I think poor Percy had tried to hide it, for it wasn't in its usual place where I'd put it on the shelf, as though he thought it might upset me. I suspect the poor man did it because he thinks the story might be taken to reflect badly on him, the man of reason and science and action, for I've noticed *Faust* and *Macbeth* were similarly hidden. Or who knows? Perhaps

Romwald secretly has censored the books to protect both of us. He's not nearly as dull and uncomprehending as you might think at first. And lately I've also gone back and reread the Greek tragedians. I know they're difficult, and somehow so distant and removed from reality, but I found myself craving them. Does that make sense?"

Catherine could see where it made a good deal of sense, but also she was quite embarrassed that a dead woman's reading list was so much more lively and sophisticated than her own. "Yes, it does. Would you like to read some books together? Are there any that you have two copies of, so we could read them at night, and discuss them in the afternoons?"

Mrs. Wallston raised her eyebrows. "You want to *read* with me?"

"Why not? You said it's what you like to do, and I like to do it too. And it'll give us something useful to talk about."

"Yes, that would be nice. Thank you."

"You're entirely welcome."

"I didn't know talking to you would be enjoyable."

"Mostly, it will be."

"And when it's not?"

"It will be useful then, too."

"That's good. Sometimes unpleasant things can be useful."

"Let's talk about which unpleasant things are useful, and which aren't."

Catherine's first real job in the craft for which she had so long and so diligently trained had finally begun. And even if it were in such a wholly unexpected way, with such an unusual and difficult charge, it was nonetheless the most thrilling, satisfying thing she had felt since she was a child.

The next several weeks continued the therapy begun that day. The hook of talking about literature rather than directly about family and personal matters was quite useful to Catherine. Though she never lost sight of the goal or the roles they must play in order for therapy to be successful, she found herself enjoying their conversations, even looking forward to them, as she looked forward to spending every evening reading the same books as Mrs. Wallston.

As Catherine had expected, the progress was much slower than Dr. Wallston could have imagined, although the physical attacks ended after the first day. But Mrs. Wallston's deep depression and anger were not dissipated, even if the outright violence had been restrained. All Catherine could offer to Dr. Wallston by way of explanation was to note that Mrs. Wallston had a deep-seated conflict with her mother, but so did practically every female of the species, so far as anyone could tell. It hardly took any new theories of Freud to ferret that out. But what lay behind those issues, the particular implications and connections of her own unique situation—these were secrets that everyone's psyche spent decades learning to hide most effectively. It hardly helped matters that Catherine could not know whether or to what extent Mrs. Wallston's mental state was affected by her physical condition and the massive quantities and unknown qualities of all the chemicals to which she was daily subjected. So, as much as Catherine enjoyed her daily work, she could make no guarantees of success, or even progress.

After several such weeks of enjoyable but inconclusive therapy, Catherine thought it was time to bring the conversation back to Mrs. Wallston's mother more explicitly than she had attempted before. Catherine was standing, as she often did in their sessions, rather than sitting, for it put them both more at ease, somehow seeming less static or formal.

"You mentioned that you did much housework when you were young. You must have had servants. Why did you have to do so much?"

Mrs. Wallston was sitting on the couch, as usual. She never lay on it, partly for the physical reason that with her system so stimulated, she was restless and had to move around constantly, thereby making lying down the more stressful and uncomfortable posture. She had also admitted, without revealing anything at all surprising, that lying down reminded her far too much of being dead again, so she avoided it. As she sometimes did, she had let her hair down after lunch, since it was just the two of them, and pins and the tightening of her scalp often annoyed her hyper-sensitized nerves. Sitting there on the dark blue sofa – her skin as always so appallingly white, accentuated by cascading folds of a dress of the same hue, and her blonde hair catching the sunlight and framing her face like the corona of an eclipse – the contrast was both unnerving and captivating, somewhat like seeing a cameo that moved and spoke.

Or, Catherine had the queerest imagining, like a large, perfect pearl set on a navy blue cushion. *Yes,* she thought, *with the sunlight spilling into the room and over her, Mrs. Wallston today has more of the pearl's iridescence than a corpse's pallor.*

Catherine couldn't quite recall the parable about the pearl, or even if there were more than one, as she could remember the Lord saying both that pearls were not to be cast before swine, but also that a pearl was of great price. As a scientist she could also not help but remember that a pearl was, in the end, little more than a giant tumor. A product of pain and nervous excitement at the most basic, animal level. Catherine thought of all these as she considered her fragile and horribly beautiful charge.

Mrs. Wallston took a deep breath, so as to say something, not because she needed to breathe. "Oh my, no, we didn't have servants. I used to think it was because mother was just being so *particular* in everything, just to spite me. And then I thought perhaps she was just being stingy, for she made my father do a lot of work around the house that a man of his stature might have expected servants to do."

Catherine nodded. "You say you used to think of those explanations. What explanation did you decide on later?"

"I remembered back to when I was very little. I remembered that then, there *were* servants, quite a few of them. A nanny, a cook, two different maids. And all of them such pretty, lively young women. All so very different… a bosomy English woman, a beautiful Irish girl, dark haired Italians, even several Negresses. Each one so different, but so charming. Several of them loved to play with me. And they all always smelled so nice… never perfume, of course, but earthy and rich and fecund, each in her own way. I loved having them near me. It was such an overwhelmingly feminine house, I don't know how my father could stand it." Mrs. Wallston wasn't really capable of laughing anymore, as it involved too much of a conscious inhaling and exhaling for it to sound like normal laughter, but she did manage a nervous sort of chuckle, almost like a cough.

"But then they were gone? Did you ever know why?"

Mrs. Wallston paused for quite a while. She frowned. She fidgeted. Catherine waited. To comfort her in her distress at this point would be premature and she would again cover up whatever it was. "They all laughed so much, too. It was quite a gay, frolicsome place. But mother never laughed. Never. I always thought her so severe and so particular and wondered why. But father laughed. He had a big, booming laugh when he was with me and we were playing. Sometimes I'd hear him behind a door, laughing with one of the servants, and it was more of a snicker. And they'd laugh then, too, but theirs weren't loud laughs, either, but more like little giggles or coos. I'd hear them behind doors and wonder. I even wondered when I actually saw him with one of them, his hands on her, lifting her skirt up, kissing her neck. I'd never seen him kiss mother that way, because one simply doesn't do that in front of others, does one?

"For a while, she'd make him dismiss just the one he'd been familiar with, but after a while, she made them all go away, once and for all. And it was father's turn to be less frolicsome and more severe. Not that mother's mood really improved. No, we were just all very dull and quiet and severe, the three of us together, after that. Oh, and we did a lot of housework. And I mean a *lot* of housework. So, no, we didn't have any servants." She attempted a very sarcastic and extremely ugly half-smile that didn't get all the way to a smirk, but stayed stuck at a snarl. "Does that answer your question?"

Catherine's next question was as predictable as it was necessary. "How did that make you feel?"

There was little pause this time. "Angry. So very, very angry. Angry at mother for making us all so miserable. And I didn't understand why she did it, of course, and later when I did, I was angry at all those women who had been so nice to me, because they weren't nice, were they? They were nasty and vicious and they ruined our lives. But do you know what? I still wanted to hold on to how they'd been nice to me, so I tried to remember just the way they smelled, because I felt that was something between us as women, all the smells we'd experienced in the kitchen and the field and the garden, all the smells that stuck to us and made us who we were, the bark and grass and lavender and leeks and nutmeg." She closed her eyes and inhaled deeply through her nose this time and smiled. Then her eyes snapped back open and she frowned again. "But I didn't want to remember their laughs, because now I could see how they'd tricked and hurt us with their nasty little tittering, being happy when they were making mother and me so sad."

Mrs. Wallston stood and walked slowly over to Catherine, enjoying the drama and control that came with revealing something that would be considered shocking and shameful, but which Mrs. Wallston knew was also powerful and captivating.

"And their necks, where I'd seen father slavering like a beast, I really couldn't stomach remembering those lovely, soft necks. Have you ever really looked at another woman's neck, doctor?" She dragged the cold fingers of her right hand along Catherine's neck for effect. It was worse than being touched by a snake, for there wasn't the solid, rubbery mass of scales backed by powerful muscle—reassuring and alive in its own way—but rather the eerie tickling of the softest skin and the scratch of sharp nails.

Every part of the caress was evacuated of all animal vitality and filled instead with the cold pain of the poor woman's intellect and memory. "A woman can be too fat or too skinny, eyes too small or too close together, nose too long or too flat or crooked, lips too thin or too thick, hips too big or legs too short. But her neck always seems to have an exquisite, unearthly beauty, as though it were carved by the greatest artist of all, which I suppose it was." She came around and leaned in very close to the right side of Catherine's neck. "I remembered all those necks, so variously lovely, and I *hated* them." She over-aspirated her words, expelling them with a pent-up passion, but the breath that seeped over and gripped Catherine's neck was as cold and dry as the exhalation of a tomb. "I *hated* them and I wanted to rip them open, with a knife, or even with my teeth. With my teeth, doctor."

Never mind the horrible and violent words, the sensation of the dead breath on Catherine's neck was even more confused and overwhelming than the cold touch. Catherine remained outwardly impassive, but she knew with a seldom-achieved clarity and certainty that, whatever else she might ever do or experience in her life, this would be the most exquisitely repulsive and erotic moment she would ever endure, rapturous and oppressive in equal and intense measure. She also realized how right Dr. Wallston had been, that the mock-divine knowledge he had uncovered did not make the real divine obsolete, but only made one realize how the primal forces of life could at any moment utterly overwhelm the paltry reason and science of man. "Are you quite sure you're not afraid of me, doctor?" Victoria rasped in Catherine's ear, her teeth all but grazing her earlobe.

Indeed, Catherine was quite sure she *was* afraid. But, as consumed with the voluptuousness of self-pity and hate as Mrs. Wallston was at that moment, and as seductive and sensuous as her witness to her own wretchedness was, Catherine was still, at some level, in control. It was finally neither eroticism nor repugnance that filled her heart, but love and compassion for another person, especially a patient she had sworn to protect and heal. She took hold of Victoria's shoulders and turned her, with all the grace and care one would a sleeping child, and gently embraced her from behind, with her right arm across the front of the dead woman's shoulders, and her cold back pressed lightly against Catherine's warm chest and beating heart. It was as erotic as Mrs. Wallston's lewd and vicious touch had just been, but also loving and maternal. And the words she whispered—with her lips actually touching the cold, dead flesh of the other woman's ear—were loving, even as they were stern. "I'm not afraid, because we both know that I'm not the real object of your rage, and neither are those women. If you could tell me I'm wrong, only then might I be afraid. So tell me what you really feel."

Catherine could feel her patient's body relax slightly, then felt the cold body shake three times, noiselessly, and she held her tighter. They hung in that embrace for what seemed a very long time, before Mrs. Wallston extricated herself and took a few steps away, turning to face her doctor again. "It's funny, really, the things you miss when you're dead. I never knew until just now how painful it would be not to have tears anymore. Isn't that funny? I should have cried more when I could, but anger was so much easier." She bowed her head slightly, then lifted it. "But now, doctor, I'm afraid I don't know how to proceed. You have lifted a heavy burden from me, but it was also in a way my *raison d'être*. What would you have me do now?"

"Now you must heal. Now you must allow yourself to be angry at the right object."

Mrs. Wallston was capable of a smirk, and one that looked much less bestial and threatening than her expressions had up until then. "My father? He's very old and lives in Providence. I hardly think I'm in any condition to travel, and I think the sight of his angry, dead daughter come to accuse him of all his sexual misdeeds might do him in once and for all. You'd give me more guilt than satisfaction or healing, doctor."

"There are ultimate causes for most everything we feel, and often those causes are far beyond our reach, but there are also proximate causes." Catherine could smirk too, and she felt more genial than she had in weeks. "I don't believe any travel will be necessary."

Catherine took her patient to Dr. Wallston's study. Mrs. Wallston knocked and opened the door herself, and he was understandably surprised to see them both. Both of them looked to Catherine for some guidance or orchestration of the event, but in reality, it really wasn't a situation for which she had trained. "Dr. Wallston," she began. "I believe we have made real progress and can now address the fundamental conflicts with which you both have been struggling."

"Splendid. Capital. When do we begin?" He stood and looked back and forth between the two of them, without a clue what was to come. Catherine had supposed he wouldn't guess what was going on, but it did make the whole thing even more awkward.

"Dr. Wallston, as I'm sure you know, much of psychoanalysis involves very delicate and unpleasant aspects of sexuality."

"Yes, I had read about it. Deep-seated complexes from childhood."

"No, not all of them, even if they are related to childhood dynamics and trauma."

"Not deep-seated? Well what, then?"

"Impulses related to present relationships. Issues of trust. And intimacy. And betrayal."

"Oh." Dr. Wallston now fidgeted. He looked sideways at his wife. "I haven't, Victoria, not once, not since early last year, before you were sick."

She looked out the window and spoke very softly. "But you *did*, Percy. And often."

"How long did you know?"

"I've always known, Percy. I can't say for certain I knew the first time, but I'm quite sure that I knew within days of the event that I had lost you. It is one of the endearing things about you, that you lack a certain deceitfulness and stealth. On the other hand, those qualities might have made our situation easier. I really don't know."

Now he turned to face her, and stepped toward her, though she remained aloof, staring out the window. "Lost me? You never lost me, Victoria, you never could. I lost my way from you. I knew I was being a beast... a horrible, lecherous beast who didn't deserve you. But I never, ever thought that you knew and that it was hurting you."

"If you did, that would be true, horrible malice, wouldn't it? As it was, it was just apathy. That, or contempt, that you thought me so absurdly stupid and unobservant. I'm not sure which is worse."

He stood next to her. "Victoria, when you became ill, all I wanted to do was cure you, so that I could be better to you, so that I could make it up to you, so that I could be as good as you are, and as good as you deserve. I have to have that chance, Victoria, or I can't live with myself. All I wanted was to be your Orpheus, only I wouldn't doubt, I wouldn't fear, I wouldn't look back. I've never looked back at my wretched past since I resolved to serve you and only you."

She turned slightly, and her colorless lips curled just slightly. "A literary allusion, Percy? Now that took real sacrifice." She looked back out the window. "But really, how can I ever feel secure or joyful with you? You found me inadequate when I was as young and beautiful as I ever will be. Now look at me!" She held her arms out, palms up, then turned them over. "I'm hideous! I imagine a ghost would be preferable, all airy and ethereal. But as it is, all your horrible, *physical* science has animated only the grossest, densest, ugliest parts of me. If I couldn't satisfy you before, I certainly will always fall far short now."

He slid his hand into hers and took it up and kissed it. "You never fell short, and you won't now, for it is your soul that is alive now. Your beautiful, fragile, pure soul. And as for your body, you are still beautiful to me, more than ever, and you will always look as you do today. It is I who will grow old and feeble, while you remain a young and strong and beautiful woman. Let me win you back. Let me always be by your side. Please. I'll do anything." He bowed his head as his voice trailed off, and Catherine had to look away. It had been voyeuristic enough, watching as long as she had. It would be downright indecent to watch him actually cry.

"No need, no need," she could hear Mrs. Wallston whisper behind her, as Catherine silently slipped from the room.

A few days later, as Romwald loaded Catherine's bags into the car, she walked out to the beautiful gardens behind the house. There was a fountain there that spilled out into a little stream that ran down the hillside to the lake below. Dr. and Mrs. Wallston were sitting on a bench by the fountain, surrounded by flowers. Drooping over them were roses as big as cabbages, while around their legs grew daisies whose blooms were as wide across as a saucer. Catherine walked over to them. In the days since their most painful and successful session, she had been helping Mrs. Wallston practice laughing, and as Catherine walked up, she could hear that she almost had it down.

They stood as she approached. Catherine smiled. "I take it some of the revivification compound needs to be disposed of, after it's been used? Is that quite safe, doctor, letting it spill out here?"

He smiled back at her as he shook her hand. "It goes through several filters and treatments first, but it does seem to have some rather pleasant effects here, doesn't it?"

Catherine watched a normal-sized bee disappear into the cavernous folds of one of the roses. "So long as I don't see any bees the size of pigeons, Dr. Wallston."

He laughed. "No, I've been watching quite closely. Just the plants right here are affected. Nothing that feeds from them, and not the plants further downstream, so the monstrosities should all be of an enjoyable nature. I also made some calls, Dr. MacGuire, and I believe when you get back to Boston, you should have much less trouble with other, less enjoyable monstrosities that live in the city, especially in the university."

"Thank you very much, Dr. Wallston. I will look forward to it."

"You're quite welcome. But it is I who must thank you. It was I who was the wretch when you arrived, not my dear wife."

"Not a wretch, doctor, but certainly wretched. You needed to see what were the 'incidentals' of life, and what was essential. So did I, for that matter, and I could not have imagined before how beautiful and complicated they were."

"Quite so." He looked at Mrs. Wallston, whose dead eyes returned the loving gaze as best they could – imperfectly, but steadfastly and unhesitatingly. If she had been like a pearl that afternoon in the sitting room, today she looked more like one of the small, white flowers on a gnarled old dogwood, after many cold and deadly winters. "As beautiful and complicated as my wife's soul." He turned to Catherine. "Goodbye, doctor. I do believe Romwald needs some help, so I'll leave you two alone."

Catherine turned to Mrs. Wallston. She had known this would happen, but she still wished she could stop or at least slow the tears flowing down her cheeks. It was just unseemly, not to mention painful. Mrs. Wallston reached up and touched the moist skin, right on the one scar she had made weeks before, and very gently took one of the drops off Catherine's cheek, balancing it on her fingertip. She held it up to the sunlight, then placed it on her own eye. She blinked, and for the first time, Catherine saw her eye sparkle, the way it must have in life.

"Catherine? May I finally call you that?" Catherine nodded. "You healed my soul, while my husband's science could only fix my body. Your skill, and most of all, your love finished what he could not. Please don't ever cry again when you think of me. I couldn't bear for my memory to bring you anything but joy, for that is what you have brought me."

"Perhaps his science was inadequate, but it was he who healed your soul as well, for it was he who had hurt it. I only helped you realize it, and gave you the strength to move on. You were the first person I ever helped heal, and that memory can only bring me the greatest joy, for the rest of my life."

They embraced, Catherine's heart again beating against Mrs. Wallston, who pressed her face into Catherine's curls and breathed her in, slowly and deliberately, sharing a love that surpassed not only sexuality, but any bodily form or limit whatsoever.

Nevermore

or

THE FEAST OF FLESH

DAVID DUNWOODY

Acknowledgements

Thanks to Jodi Lee and Belfire: for originally bringing this story to un-life, and for making un-life look so damn good.

NEVERMORE

Malcolm Witt died in his sleep at 11:07 PM. Four minutes later, his body rose and walked from the room. Malcolm watched it happen.

6:25 PM

He was nervous enough as it was, and it showed—in his flinching countenance, in the way his fingers danced restlessly on the steering wheel, in the way his tightly-wound gut pulled him forward in his seat and the way he kept his upper arms pressed to his sides, fearing sweat. His mood was evident enough already, and the cloying dampness in the air was making it worse. Regardless of his composure, a sheen was forming on his brow. *Maybe,* he thought, *the air will have the same effect on everyone else.*

He was sure he'd be the only one under scrutiny. His stomach made another quarter-turn, and he was nearly hunched over the wheel.

It had been threatening to rain all day. The slate-gray sky was now mottled with black bruises, and Malcolm knew it would be pouring by nightfall. "So there's that to look forward to."

"I'll drive home," his brother told him. "Relax."

"I know there's nothing to be upset about. Not now. What's the point? I *know* that, but I'm ready to come apart."

"He won't even be there." Ray patted him on the shoulder. "You know, you didn't let on how worked up you were over this."

"I didn't think I was," Malcolm sighed. "And by the way, I'm sorry we're going straight from the airport to dinner. It's just not as easy as it used to be to get people together."

"No worries," Ray said. "It'll be a nice time. I'm looking forward to it. I want you to have a drink and mellow out. Or two. I'm driving home. Okay?"

Big brother never failed to come through. Malcolm's tension eased, if only a little.

Malcolm's circle of friends was modest, and it had been over a month since he'd seen most of them. There had been e-mails and phone calls offering their encouragement, of course, but it was increasingly difficult to get more than a couple of them together at once, even on a Friday night. He knew that was just due to work schedules, but it had been eating at him nonetheless—especially because Leo made his own hours, and could see anyone anytime he wanted—and so Malcolm had become determined to have an evening out.

And Leo won't *be there,* he reminded himself. Leo didn't even know, according to Bonnie. Being part of such subterfuge at thirty-five years of age felt a bit ridiculous, but he told himself it was only temporary. They'd speak eventually, awkward overtures would be made, and mea culpas accepted. They'd find something stupid to laugh about and then these awful boundaries could be dissolved. *That's what we both really want, I'm sure. Maybe he'll even make the first move.*

Malcolm pulled into the parking lot of the Arthur Arms. "They have an Arms in Portland," Ray said, "and it sucks. Have I told you that before?"

"Probably." Malcolm killed the engine. He straightened his jacket and appraised himself in the mirror. He wanted them to tell Leo he'd looked good. He'd knock back a couple of drinks and tell some jokes. God, he hadn't felt so much as a pang of grief in five weeks, and now this. He supposed he hadn't thought about how the breakup might affect other relationships.

"I think we go *inside* the restaurant," said Ray.

"All right, all right." Malcolm threw open his door. Cool air kissed his face and, for just a second, he thought of the thin blue lips of a corpse. At their mother's viewing, he and Ray had both noticed that she was wearing the wrong shade of lipstick. It had looked cakey and absurd, like chalk on the mouth of a mannequin.

Bonnie was the only one there so far, and she rose to hug both men as they approached the booth. It was set into an oak-paneled alcove with mood lighting, far from the boisterous activity at the bar. "Thank you," Malcolm told her.

Bonnie slipped back into the rear of the circular booth. Giving them a look of mock reproach, she said, "Well, at least you're not the last to arrive."

"My fault," Ray told her. "It was my flight. But you got us a great spot."

"Did you put it under my name?" Malcolm asked. Bonnie shook her head. "Oh. I don't think either Jean or Saul know your last name," he said. "I'd better—"

"I got it," Ray slid out of the booth.

Bonnie's eyes flitted from him to Malcolm. "Does he age at all?"

"Hey." He pointed at her. "I need you to focus."

"I'm still here for you," she said. "I can multitask."

"Seriously. Ray's not doing anything until Monday. Ask him out tomorrow."

"Very well." She folded her hands and gave him her full attention. "So, what've you been doing with yourself?"

"Not much," he said, apologetically, but she was listening. "I go to work, I come home and do lesson plans, I go to bed. I go crazy. I call you."

"You could call me more often," she said.

"It's just been weird."

"I know."

Ray returned to the table. "Put it under Witt. So Bon, what's new?"

"Business as usual," she told him. Casting a glance at Malcolm, she said softly, "I'm not allowed to talk about it."

"Oh, stop." Malcolm waved in at the bar, trying to catch a server's eye.

Ray laughed. "Maybe we could get into it later," he said to Bonnie.

"Guys—" Malcolm began.

"It's fine." Ray gave him a reassuring smile.

Someone bumped against Malcolm's arm, and he looked up, expecting a waitress; but it was a thin man with shoulder-length blond hair. He set a tumbler of Scotch before Malcolm. "I made it a double."

"How long have you been here?" Malcolm asked with a wry smile.

The man seated himself beside Malcolm with his own drink in hand, saying nothing. The short-haired man who'd accompanied him to the booth said, "Forgive Jean, he assumes everyone already knows who he is." The man extended his hand to Ray. "Jordan Saul."

"Ray Witt. Nice to make your acquaintance." Ray moved closer to Bonnie so that Saul could join them. Jean, perched on the edge of the seat next to Malcolm, raised his glass in an unknown toast and drained its contents.

"Jean Haniver," Malcolm finally told Ray. "Let's not interrupt his entrance. It should be over by the third drink." Jean didn't respond even to that. Swallowing a mouthful of Scotch, Malcolm elbowed him. "Ray's my brother."

Jean thrust his hand across the table. "Ray Witt. Two years Colmy's senior, single, and a lawyer. You're here for the Old Valley hearing. Representing the tree-huggers."

Ray grinned. "Close. Very close. 'Colmy' and I are three years apart."

Jean raised an eyebrow and turned to Malcolm. "So you really *are* thirty-five." He flagged down a passing waitress and held up his glass. "This is a vodka tonic." To the booth he said, "Sorry about the rudeness of my 'entrance.' I was getting a read on Ray. Didn't even know Malcolm had a brother. Could have skipped the routine if he'd simply told me—*and* introduced me as Jean Haniver, psychic."

It was true, Jean had pulled every fact he knew about Ray from thin air, though they were all adults seated at the table, and he must have deduced it from simple observation. Jean could have made an honest living in some science instead of the Sylvia Browne shtick, but then he probably wouldn't have had the books or the TV appearances or the seminars.

It was hard to believe Saul had mentored him. The two had never been lovers, as far as Malcolm knew, but had worked closely for years. Saul had been a nightclub magician at the height of his career; now semi-retired and managing Jean, he still pulled a bit of sleight-of-hand at parties, but stayed away from interpreting messages from the Great Spirit World. *True magic is far too grim for me,* Saul was fond of saying. *I much prefer card tricks.*

Malcolm caught his eye and smiled. When Saul smiled back, Malcolm could see the silver in his beard. He knew Saul had to be much older than he looked. Malcolm supposed that was a bit of real-world magic at work.

When the waitress returned with Jean's refill, they ordered their entrees. "I thought you would've already known about Ray," Bonnie said to Jean with jovial sarcasm.

"I never go where I'm not invited," Jean said, and tapped his forefinger against Malcolm's temple. He swayed, just slightly, and again Malcolm wondered how long he and Saul had been seated at the bar.

"I am an attorney, though," Ray said. "You nailed that. Knowing that much, you could have guessed I flew in for Old Valley, but how did you get attorney in the first place?"

"A magician never...well, you know." Jean waved off the question.

Saul crossed his arms with his typical bemused expression.

Malcolm's belly was warm with Scotch, and the muscles in his stomach and chest had relaxed. He went through another Scotch and most of his manicotti without thought. Things were going just as he'd hoped.

Ray went on a little spiel about Old Valley, the storm-water treatment plant that the city had shut down and sold off. The developer was allegedly using it for illegal dumping. "It hasn't been processed at all like it was supposed to be, and there are still lines that haven't been sealed. That toxic swamp is already backing up into the new system, I guarantee it."

Bonnie set her fork down beside a half-finished steak. "Delightful."

"Sorry," Ray said, "I know it's not dinner conversation." He leaned over to her. "Let's pick it up tomorrow at lunch. I've got a whole rap on raw sewage."

"Yummy." But the invitation had clearly made her night. Having come down from his anxiety, Malcolm was able to appreciate the moment.

"Bonnie and I graduated from Gibson together," Ray told Saul and Jean. "Never really dated. Well, we kinda did. Whatever happened?"

"Your rotten little brother wouldn't leave us alone," Bonnie shot back. Malcolm laughed hardest of all.

"You two are in love," Jean said abruptly. The laughter in the booth died. "Well," he shrugged, "you are."

Malcolm was surprised Jean hadn't really leapt for the brass ring, and offered to divine the identity of the man Leo had slept with; then again, he probably already knew. And with that, Malcolm's emotions bottomed out and his mind left the room.

"Hey," Ray said, then again. "Hey—you still with us?"

Malcolm threw the rest of his drink down his gullet. "I'll be back," he said, and motioned for Jean to move out of the booth so he could get up. The psychic huffed at having his performance interrupted, but Malcolm heard him go right back into character the moment he walked away. *So much for friends.* But he'd wanted things to go on as they always had, right? He was the one being fickle. He pushed through the men's room door and situated himself before the urinal. Another drink, maybe, when he got back.

When he walked out of the restroom, Jean was waiting in the Arms' entryway. "You're clearly a mess."

"You've done it again." Malcolm gave him a thumbs-up.

"Really. You've tried to go on like Leo just stopped existing, but no one's buying it. Have you talked to him at all?"

It sounded like there might be genuine concern in Jean's voice. Malcolm softened a bit. "Not since he told me." He raised his eyebrows. "I don't want to know anything, Jean. Not from you."

"Who says I know?" Jean shrugged. "Leo hasn't said a thing. And I don't think he will."

Malcolm really didn't want to know who it had been. But he'd always known it might have been a mutual acquaintance, and upon hearing that Leo still hadn't disclosed the name, Malcolm's heart sank. Had to be a friend. Perhaps even someone who had offered their sympathies over the past five weeks.

It had been two months after it happened before Leo told Malcolm. In hindsight, he had spent those months building up to it—making confessions in the form of what-ifs or would-yous. All the hypotheticals, even accusations, but Malcolm hadn't wanted to see it. More so, perhaps, he hadn't believed it was *possible.*

Yes, things had cooled between them, and both had acknowledged that, but he hadn't known it was over. That was just it—it *hadn't* been over, not until Leo's drunken call. He'd been in a tearful panic, and Malcolm had at first been concerned, but Leo's insistence on coming over before he explained what was wrong had been what did it.

Malcolm had known then, and had said, "Tell me now or I'm hanging up. Tell me now, or I won't talk to you again."

"Malcolm, *please!*"

"Tell me!"

And he had. And Malcolm had hung up.

"Listen," Jean said softly. "I'm not going to mess around in Leo's head. But you deserve to know. There are things I can do to help you—"

"For Christ's sake, *don't,*" Malcolm snapped. "Treat me with some goddamn respect."

Jean flinched away. "I mean it. I can help you see."

Jean was only making him angrier at Leo. That it had come to this! The thought of overtures and mea culpas was heading right out the window. Still the man persisted. "You know I mean it!"

"I don't think I know anything about you."

"How will you find out the name, then? Your lawyer brother? Or maybe Bonnie? She's a cop, right? She can look into it." He snorted. "Do you get what I'm saying? I have the tools for this work, and I'm willing to use them. As a friend, Malcolm."

He just couldn't stand being told no. He preyed on desperate hope. Malcolm walked past him and out of the restaurant.

"Where are you going?"

"Smoke," he said, probably too low for Jean to hear, but he didn't care.

It was dark, but the rain hadn't yet come. As Malcolm crossed the parking lot, pulling out a near-empty pack of Marlboros, he heard a voice call: "You said you were quitting."

Saul smiled in the halo of light from his Bic. "Same to you," Malcolm said, and went over.

"Well, it was true when I said it." Saul offered the flame to him. "Jean followed me out to wait for you...did you talk?"

"Yeah. I guess he's trying to help, in his way. I'd prefer he didn't." Malcolm shoved his hands into his pockets and stared at the blacktop. "I was actually starting to appreciate how oblivious he can be."

Saul coughed and leaned against his Taurus. Some wit had printed WASH ME on the dusty door, and he struck the words out with his fingertips. "Well, I'm no greater a sage than he."

"I know," Malcolm said. "Still thought I'd ask - why are we here?"

"Nature abhors a vacuum." Headlights panned over Saul's smile and vanished into the night.

Malcolm wished he could ask a real question, but he knew Saul didn't like playing the role of wise King Solomon. Saul loathed stereotypes as much as he did—and Jean was bad enough for both of them—but Malcolm had always looked up to him in some way, and had envied that mentor relationship with Jean. He tried to emulate it with his students. Most of them didn't need it, though. They had dads and all the rest of it.

Didn't I promise myself one more drink? Malcolm stubbed his cigarette out on the asphalt and picked up the crumpled butt. "Want to head back in?"

"Sounds good." Saul pinched his cigarette between his thumb and forefinger. Malcolm stopped. Saul winked at him. Then the cigarette was gone.

Jean was back in the booth with Ray and Bonnie, and pointed sideways at the tumbler by Malcolm's plate. "Got you another."

"Thanks." Malcolm sat down beside him. "Really."

"Least I could do."

Ray and Bonnie were on their second round, and had moved closer to one another. Malcolm reached for his drink, but Jean turned and dropped a finger into it.

"What are you...?"

Jean placed his wet finger against Malcolm's forehead and swirled it. It felt like he was writing something. "What are you doing?" Malcolm murmured.

"Lensing your third eye. For sight."

Malcolm swatted his hand away angrily. "You're fucking impossible."

Jean didn't react to his glower, merely pushed the glass toward him and said, "Have at it then."

Just for that, Malcolm took a thick gulp. It tasted slightly sweet. He looked into the glass. "What's with this?"

"It's scotch." Jean looked at him. "What do you see?"

"I see you," Malcolm muttered.

"Hmm." Jean sat back and yawned. "I am very drunk."

"You good to drive?" Malcolm asked Ray.

"Sure. You ready to call it a night, then?"

"I think so." Malcolm got up and fished for his wallet. "I had a nice time. I did. It's fine."

"I'm going to come by tomorrow," Bonnie said, but Malcolm knew she was coming for Ray, and offered only a sullen nod in response.

The sky split the moment they walked outside. Malcolm was soaked to the bone before he made it to the car.

"Are you really okay?" Ray asked.

"As good as it gets." Malcolm fell onto his bed and pressed his palms to his temples. "You sure about taking the couch?"

"I sleep on the couch in my office most nights," Ray said. "Do you drink that much very often?"

"Never again," was all Malcolm said. "Never again."

The door closed. "Never again," he whispered, and slipped into a sea of black clouds.

11:07 PM

His first awareness was of the fact that he was dead.

It was a simple truth, and he could not articulate in his thoughts how he knew, except that he knew he was nothing *but* thought. There was no sensation. The darkness of sleep had given way to a storm of white light, light he wasn't really seeing so much as he was being permeated by it. What substance he had was less than a mote, and the light had absorbed him.

He knew he was dead, but he didn't know where he was, or if *here* was even a place. There was no point of reference, no sense of orientation. Maybe he didn't exist in places anymore. Maybe he was reduced to something that had no fixture in any dimension. Maybe he had joined a great nothing.

But the light was there, and it was real, and then there came a dull sense of something behind the light, a rising cacophony that unsettled his awareness. He couldn't concentrate on whatever it was, couldn't discern its nature or source. All was chaos. If he could have, Malcolm would have screamed.

No senses. No body. He was suddenly keenly aware of the lack of *Malcolm*. No prickling flesh, no tired bones, no pulsing veins or swelling lungs. There was no pounding heart or surging adrenaline. He supposed that was why he felt so still despite his utter confusion.

But that thrumming chaos was building around him, and unease was growing in his being. It was a discordant sea of sound—*sound!* It was sound he perceived, vibrations bombarding him from every direction, as with the light. The sound of the living world. He had it now: a ticking clock. The settling building. The changing pressure in the walls. Mites scrabbling through carpet fibers. And falling rain.

He focused on the rain, giving him a point of reference. Rain on the roof overhead. Slowly but surely, those less significant noises retreated into the background. It felt like he was really hearing the rain now. And the particles of light about him began to fade.

His mental focus was giving him sight now. He recognized the outlines of his bedroom. His perspective was at eye level, as if he still had eyes in a head on a body. And, though his focus was narrowing, he sensed that he had a full 360-degree view of the room, if he wanted it. Malcolm wondered at it all. If he'd been screaming, the scream would have died, and been replaced by a gentle, disbelieving laugh.

He was at the foot of his bed, and there before him lay his dead body.

The clock read nine past eleven. He wondered how long he had been dead. Time seemed as alien to him now as gravity or temperature. As alien as the sack of flesh lying prone on the bed. For the first time he saw himself as others must have. His still-clothed body lay atop the covers, and he was able to appraise its form without relating it to himself.

There were jowls, which formed with his head propped up on the pillows, and settled against a neck that he'd thought was thick but seemed slight and frail beneath that bloated head. His hair was big and messy and sat on his scalp like a toupee. He'd had beautiful eyelashes, at least, and nice hands. One lay to the left of his head, palm turned upward, fingers half-closed.

Malcolm studied his dead face. It was pale, waxy. Reminded him of something, or someone. His former skin glistened with shrinking beads of sweat. He couldn't have been gone long.

At 11:11 his body sat up.

Malcolm was frozen in place. He wanted to leap back, to push himself away from the staring face that had once been his own, but he couldn't. There was no way to move, no physiology—he was trapped! Fear swelled in him, pure emotional terror—and unfiltered light and sound began encroaching on him once more as he lost focus. He could still see the body, rising now to stand beside the bed, limbs stiff, eyes unblinking. How? Everything else seemed to make sense, but this was wrong, he knew it with absolute certainty. *How?*

The body walked to the door and fumbled awkwardly with the knob. The door opened just wide enough for it to push through. Malcolm lost sight of it, as he was losing sight of everything...

Ray!

He tore through the distortion and was back in the room. And, distantly, he felt something like feet planted on the floor beneath him. It was another dull impression, but it was certain. He was standing on the floor, and though he saw no feet there, nor were any of the carpet's threads flattened by any sort of weight, he did see *something*. Two somethings. Dark, glistening stains, like footprints.

He heard his brother murmur his name. It sounded as if he'd just been roused from sleep.

And then Ray screamed.

Malcolm tried to move but there was nothing *to* move. He'd reconnected to the physical, now how was he supposed to pull himself across its plane? *Ray! RAY!*

Ray let out a terrible, wounded yell, a sound Malcolm had never heard from his older brother. And whatever was happening, that walking corpse was doing it—did Ray think it was Malcolm himself? Of course he did! Meanwhile Malcolm was frozen in space mere feet away! *RAY!*

He looked at the floor again. In the air between his point of view and the stains on the floor, he saw other dark splotches simply hovering. He realized he was looking at the backs of two dangling hands. How was he giving form to himself? How did he use it? Ray sputtered and cried, *"Mal—"*

A wet, heavy sound. Then silence.

He didn't know what this dark matter on his surface was— didn't know what his surface was—but it was eroding before his sight and he felt as if he were coming un-tethered from the world. Light swelled around him again. *Focus!*

He focused on Ray, and the shadows of the room returned. He thought about Ray, not about what state he might be in, but getting to him, and he sensed feet on carpet again. He saw dark syrup pooling in the air beneath him. He saw strange, thin limbs taking shape as the syrup spread—legs, not fully realized, but enough to give him confidence. He tried to take a step. Nothing happened.

No. You can't walk. That's not how it works.

His focus had generated this weird substance where he imagined his legs and feet to be, so he focused himself forward. And he was fifteen inches closer to the door.

All right. Don't let emotion overcome you. Just focus. Forward.

He came right up to the door. There was no sound from the next room; he heard only the driving rain. Malcolm looked at the doorknob. Could he take hold of it, or even just push against the wood?

He focused on the door. Dark stains appeared there. They looked vaguely green in the light from the street. But nothing else happened. *God damn you*...again he cast his focus upon the door, and fresh stains appeared, only to evaporate. He couldn't seem to affect any movement at all. And why should he have expected otherwise? He couldn't apply any real force to it, could he? He searched his memory. He taught—*had* taught—social studies, not science. Like it really made a difference, he was a ghost trying to go through a door.

I'm a ghost.

He focused himself through the wood and into the living room.

Ray lay on the couch, arms above his head, one foot on the floor. His eyes were open. His mouth was a gaping, bloody hole, his shattered jaw hanging slack. He was dead. Murdered. The front door lay open.

Malcolm lost the world again. He recoiled into the light so that it blinded him, and the cacophonous sounds that enveloped him were as his screams.

The wall clock by the window said it was almost 11:30, but it felt as if only a few minutes had passed since Malcolm's own death, or his awareness of it. It seemed he was losing time whenever he became disoriented. He had no idea how long it had taken Ray to die while he was in the bedroom.

There was blood everywhere. Parts of Ray were missing. His right leg ended at the knee. Malcolm could only react with silent grief, unable to turn away or retch or weep.

My brother is dead. But so am I.

He scanned the room. *Ray? Are you here?*

He wasn't. One way or another, Ray was just gone.

Why am I still here? It had to have something to do with the state of his body. The cadaver's eyes had been blank, but had seen right through Malcolm to the door. To Ray. And it had gone to him, and killed him. *WHY?*

The idea struck Malcolm that his body was now an unmanned vessel: soulless, feral. That this might be the natural state of a human organism, deprived of its spiritual host, didn't quell his confusion. Perhaps that was an explanation for the cadaver's behavior, but it still didn't explain why it was walking around to begin with. Ray's remains were dead as could be, and Ray's spirit was absent. It had to be that Malcolm was somehow still tied to his body, allowing it to run on fumes, so to speak, while he could only watch.

An out-of-body experience gone too far? Could we be rejoined?

No. He didn't want that, not now. But he wanted to remedy whatever nightmarish error had been committed by the universe. He sensed he was alone in this, and so he focused on the front door and moved into the dark hallway.

The corridor connecting the apartments was always dimly-lit, and he could see splashes of blood on the floor and the walls— those on the walls prominently displaying the details of his fingers. He focused ahead, and now could see that the substance he was casting—*ectoplasm?*—was indeed green in color. The amorphous prints of his pseudo-feet were stamped into the bloodstains, only to erode seconds later. He proceeded down the hall and into the stairwell.

How to do this, then, without gravity? He focused on each step in turn, casting the ectoplasm down, and found himself being pulled along with it. It was getting easier. As long as he kept himself calm, he was in control.

He entered the narrow lobby of the building and stared through its glass entryway into the storm. There was a red handprint on the outer door. On the floor, just inside the building, lay the rest of Ray's leg. It looked as if the meat had been peeled from the bone in strips. Malcolm, realizing where the meat had gone, nearly lost it again.

Focus! He went to the door. The rain was still coming down hard, the vibrations were overwhelming. *It might be difficult to move out there.* But he knew it was possible; he went through the glass.

The light from the streetlamps danced through each drop of rain as it slashed downward, lancing through him and slapping against the side of the building. Looking at the steps, he slowly made his way down. He'd thought the sound might make it harder to focus and move, but it was the rain itself that was the problem—, washing away the ectoplasm almost as soon as he cast it, forcing him to cast more and more to cover the short distance. Once on the sidewalk, he looked in either direction. No cars, no people. No cadaver.

Wait—there it is, standing in the middle of the intersection at 16th and Westmore. Its back was to him, and it stared up at the traffic light as the caution signal blinked. *Clap, clap, clap.*

Malcolm stayed on the sidewalk as he advanced toward the cadaver. He knew he didn't need to, but concentrating was difficult enough without the possibility of a car ripping through him. If a car plowed into the corpse, would it die? Would it be injured at all?

He stopped at the corner of the intersection. The thing turned slightly, and Malcolm watched as blood was washed from its gaping mouth. It didn't seem to be looking directly at him, but he feared it might sense his presence. No way of knowing.

Then it staggered toward him. Malcolm was fixed in place. He didn't know what to do. He didn't know if it could hurt him—

The cadaver stepped through Malcolm, without trauma or sensation, and it headed down Westmore. The ghost-Malcolm reversed himself and followed after it. He supposed he couldn't be hurt anymore.

Besides his father, Leo was the only one who'd done it to him. He'd told Leo that he could—he'd revealed his vulnerability sometime early in their four-year relationship, in three words. Leo had said the words back, and Malcolm believed he'd meant them. So why end things they way he had—why destroy any chance of salvaging the friendship they'd built upon?

Leo was six years younger than Malcolm. He'd been twenty-five when they met, brilliant and angry and defying anyone to try to slow him on his reckless path. Malcolm supposed he'd wanted to guide Leo at first, but there was nothing doing. Leo had been Jean Haniver's friend, and shared his appetite for chaos. Still Malcolm had persisted. It had resulted in some fiery arguments, and that at last had opened Leo's heart.

He'd had a cancer scare as a child. At the age when most kids were learning the truth about Santa or trying to make sense of a grandparent's passing, Leo had lived in Death's shadow. He knew that was the source of his anger and his fuck-it attitude, but knowing didn't change anything. In the end, neither had Malcolm.

No, ending things civilly wasn't Leo's style. He'd driven them into a wall. Malcolm, up until the moment of his death, had not known just how they could rebuild any sort of friendship—it was what he wanted, what he hoped Leo wanted, but he couldn't write off the betrayal. So, five weeks of silence. Of course he'd had many a tearful revelation, and rehearsed countless grim summations alone in his room. But, he had hung up on Leo that night, had shut him out, and he'd kept it that way. At any rate, he could have extracted no amount of suffering from Leo that would have tempered his own.

The cadaver stopped halfway down the block. More colored lights—the strobing red and blue of a police cruiser—were approaching. The dead thing stood and waited as the car pulled over to the curb. Malcolm didn't feel hope, only dread, as he watched the two officers get out from either side. The driver, a female, called to the cadaver. "You okay there?" To them, Malcolm's former body must have looked like that of a strung-out addict, soaked and staring dumbly ahead.

The female cop was half-inside the car, trying to shelter herself from the rain as she spoke into her radio. The male on the passenger side came around the front of the cruiser. "Why don't we get you out of the rain, buddy?"

The cadaver's eyes met his. The cop's mouth opened, and his body tensed, but the cadaver was already in motion and then its hands were on his head. The cadaver's own head plunged forward, like that of a spurned lover after one last violent kiss. It missed most of the cop's mouth, though, instead biting into his lip and cheek, tearing away a mouthful of flesh.

Malcolm could only watch.

The female cop stumbled out of the cruiser at the sound of her partner's shrieking. The cadaver clamped its jaws over the man's nose and left eye. Both officers were screaming now, as the cadaver's teeth scissored through muscle and cartilage and slowly pulled free a thick strip of the man's face.

The female drew her sidearm. She babbled incoherence and pointed the weapon at the cadaver, who ignored her. *"STOOOP!"* she screamed, and fired.

The bullet ripped across the backs of the cadaver's shoulders. Malcolm heard it buzz past him. *Run,* he urged the cop. *Just run!*

She didn't. The cadaver released the male cop, who fell against the hood of the cruiser and splashed down in the gutter. The corpse turned to her; she fired again, right through its heart. The cadaver stumbled a bit, the regained its footing. Malcolm tried to focus on the sidewalk ahead. *Have to get between them. Have to* do *something.*

The cadaver seized both of the woman's wrists and pulled her into a crushing embrace. She turned her head away, pleading—it bit into her ear. Malcolm heard it grunt as it ripped at her. The gun went off again, then dropped onto the concrete. The cadaver wrestled the cop toward a narrow alleyway between two brownstones. *Fuck!* Malcolm cast himself after them. Then he heard a sputtering from the street.

The other cop sat up, the left side of his face a yawning crater. Blood pulsed from it and spilled down the front of his uniform in rivers. He seemed to be in shock, staring through Malcolm at the alley, then he was looking *at* Malcolm. The ghost was certain of it. He didn't know what to do. *I'm so sorry. It's not my fault.* Ectoplasm formed in air—two reaching hands, Malcolm's hands—and was disintegrated in the rain.

The cop fell back and was still. Their gazes had met in the moment of death, now he was gone.

Malcolm moved into the pitch-dark alley. He tried to pick apart the mess of sounds bouncing off the walls. There, a soft grunting, a whimper. A crunch.

He made out the cadaver, kneeling over the woman. Her jacket and shirt lay open, and the cadaver was methodically peeling sheets of flesh from her chest and belly. It lifted its head to stuff each piece in turn into its maw. The cadaver's face was flushed, eyes bulging, it was starting to not look like Malcolm anymore. It was an animal, crude and ugly. Malcolm moved closer, *if only I could take hold of the wretched thing, I'd tear it to pieces.* And not in the slow, measured way it was taking apart the cop. No, he would spill its entrails on the asphalt and stomp its skull to dust. He was starting to feel overwhelmed again, but he could hardly calm himself.

The cadaver stood. They were face to face now; he wanted the thing to see him. He wanted it to fear and loathe *him* as he did *it*. But its eyes were vacant, its fingers probed at its ruddy cheeks, then brushed away the hair plastered on its brow.

And then its fingers curled, tearing into the flesh. It started to peel back its own scalp. The skin of its face and neck was suffused with blood now, and its head was more bloated than ever. The scalp fell against the back of its head and hung there.

It hooked its fingers beneath its jaw-line and started to remove the face. The dermis separated from the body like the peel of an orange. It was like the cadaver was *molting*, and what was beneath barely resembled Malcolm at all. It was raw and dark and patches of bone showed through. All the while rain spilled over the unblinking globes of its eyes.

Scant inches from the horror, Malcolm saw something etched in the fibrous tissue over the forehead. It was like a deep, smooth scar, something that didn't belong—in fact, it looked like a *design*, a symbol—then it began to glow like a fiery brand.

"*What are you doing?*"
"*Lensing your third eye. For sight.*"

He remembered Jean's finger tracing across his brow, remembered the way it had swirled and darted. He had dipped his finger in Malcolm's scotch, which had tasted strangely sweet, and he had asked Malcolm: "*What do you see?*"

"*I see you.*"

Jean Haniver, Leo's dearest and oldest friend.

Malcolm shot back from the cadaver, out of the alleyway, and focused through the storm. Jean didn't live far. Malcolm wondered if he was asleep. Wondered if he was alone.

He went to find out.

He thought about Leo, then Ray, then Leo again. Malcolm was forced to stop several times to orient himself, he had to focus on what he knew. Just the facts—there weren't many—he was certain Jean had put something in his drink, he knew Jean had authored the obscene symbol he could see on the cadaver's head, and he had an idea of why.

Surely Leo didn't know, he wouldn't have been complicit in murder. As far as Malcolm was aware, Leo hadn't even known about the dinner... but Jean *was* the other man, had to be. Once again, Malcolm had overlooked the obvious and given Leo the benefit of the doubt.

So Jean had some semblance of a motive—didn't want Malcolm to find out about them, and interfere—and he was evidently more desperate than Malcolm ever imagined.

But things were still fragmented. Why had he done what he'd done to Malcolm's body? Hadn't it been enough just to destroy Malcolm? Didn't this madness threaten to expose Jean?

Maybe he'd fucked up. Maybe it was just that simple.

Malcolm passed through the door of Jean's townhouse, and stood in a darkened living room decorated with garish charcoal prints from one of Jean's other friends. Intertwined demons glared down at Malcolm from all sides. He crossed the room, glancing at the books on the coffee table—all Jean's, save for a magazine that was open to an article titled "Negative Prophet." Looked like a skeptic's treatise on Jean's "work." Malcolm imagined a smile at that, then went to the stairs.

Going up is probably going to be harder than going down. He cast his focus onto the first step, and was pulled forward. No problem at all. He supposed it was all the same to him, he could probably walk on walls if he wanted to. He wished Jean could see him. He'd love to appear on the ceiling over the bastard's head and give him a goddamn heart attack.

That gave him pause. How had he supposed to communicate with Jean at all? He looked at the ectoplasm evaporating beneath him. If he could cast it in a more controlled manner, then maybe that, too, would prove easier than he thought.

It has to be easy. If Jean is able to speak with spirits, there can't be much heavy lifting involved.

Standing in the upstairs hall, before what he presumed to be the bedroom door, Malcolm steeled himself. What would he do if Leo was here?

I'll tell him.

He went in.

Jean was alone, fast asleep under Egyptian cotton, arms and legs splayed over the width of the bed. Malcolm stood over him and stared for a time, thinking about how he could awaken him. He didn't think he could touch him, nor knock anything over. He focused on Jean's placid expression and drew closer. He thought of Jean's finger dipping into the scotch, and willed his own finger into existence, a green-tinged digit hovering right over Jean's forehead. Casting the finger downward, he touched Jean's flesh. It was an oddly detached sensation, as if his own skin—had he any—were numbed by anesthetic. He drew a clumsy X there, then watched as it faded.

Jean shivered, stirred. His eyelids fluttered. "Mrm." Then his eyes opened. Malcolm stared down into them, watched as they explored the dark room, as Jean tried to recall what had roused him.

Malcolm traced another X on Jean's cheek. The man rolled away, swiping at his face with an irritated grunt. Jean was facing the window now, and Malcolm saw a humidifier on the bureau there, and condensation on the rain-streaked glass. He thought of the words WASH ME printed on Saul's car, and he moved to it and raised his finger to the glass.

Perhaps Jean couldn't see the ectoplasm, but he'd see the letters being drawn in the moisture.

He'd see *H E L L O.*

Jean sat up with a scream., his arms shrank to his sides, and he stared, trembling, at the window. The letters were gradually obscured by fresh moisture. Malcolm wrote HELLO again.

"Wha..." Jean shook his head. "What? No!"

He didn't seem at all like the veteran psychic Malcolm had witnessed in the past. Had he only summoned the spirits himself before now? Was Malcolm his first uninvited guest?

HELLO JEAN

"What!" Jean's nude form leapt from the bed and backed toward the door. "What is this—who are you?"

The first letters began to fade before Malcolm finished his name, but Jean understood well enough. "Malcolm... Malcolm *Witt?*"

YOU KILLED ME

"What?" Jean grabbed the doorknob. Malcolm scribbled a big NO on the glass.

"What do you want?" Jean screamed.

YOU KILLED ME

"I didn't kill anyone! What are you talking about?"

3RD EYE, Malcolm wrote.

Jean frowned. "Malcolm—it's really you? You're *dead?* How are you dead?"

SCOTCH

POISON

YOU

"I would never—!" Jean was suddenly aware of his nakedness, and his hands flew to his crotch. "Malcolm, I didn't do anything! You have to believe me!"

PUT IN MY DRINK. The words appeared and faded, one after the other.

"Put something in your drink? No! I mean—"

WHAT?

"Jesus Christ Malcolm, all I did was give you a little Yellow Sign! I've done it with people before. It's harmless. It just helps you to see!"

WHAT IS YELLOW SIGN

"It's just a syrup with some herbs. I learned to make it in New Bedlam when I studied with Saul. It's for lensing the third eye, just like I told you."

This Yellow Sign had to be the reason for the cadaver. And it had to be what had killed Malcolm. Jean was lying about its purpose, if not its origin. Malcolm wrote: LIAR

"No! I swear to Christ! Ask Saul!" Jean moved toward the phone on the bedside table.

CALL LEO, Malcolm wrote.

"Why would I call Leo? He doesn't know."

HE SHOULD KNOW WHAT YOU DID

"I didn't do fucking anything!" Jean shouted. "And I don't even know where the fuck Leo is! I told you I don't know who this fucking guy is!"

Malcolm hesitated at the glass. Jean was claiming he wasn't the one?

Jean fell on his knees by the bed. He sobbed, "I've never hurt anyone. Not like that! I know you hate what I do, everyone does! But I—I—I can't even fucking talk to spirits, Malcolm!" His tone was furious. "Yeah, it's all bullshit. Are you fucking happy now?!"

The window didn't respond. "Are you here?" Jean whispered. "Malcolm?"

CALL SAUL

"I will!" Jean practically knocked the phone from the table as he dove for it. "He'll tell you. He can do things. Real things. Maybe even..." He looked up. "Maybe he can even see you."

Jean dialed. Malcolm waited.

"Saul? Saul, it's me. It's after one. Listen, I need to come over. Something's happened. Mal—there's a spirit here. I mean it this time. Please let me come over."

Jean lowered the phone. "I...how will we get there? I mean, how will you get there?" He was talking to Malcolm. "Can you just, like teleport, or—"

WALK

"Walk?" Jean almost laughed.

WE'LL WALK

"All right. Okay. Whatever you want. Saul will straighten this out. He'll know what to do." Jean went to the closet and fumbled through his clothes. "You'll see, Malcolm. You believe me, right?" He turned to the window. "I'm a good person."

Malcolm didn't write anything. Jean quietly got dressed.

They walked together through the rain, Jean constantly glancing around himself, as if he might catch a glimpse of Malcolm's form, constantly asking, "You're there, aren't you? Are you there? Saul needs to see you."

Malcolm knew he was still lying about something, just not what. He stalked Jean through the rain, listening to his coughs and complaints. Like Jean said, Saul would straighten it out.

He thought of the cadaver and saw the glowing symbol in his mind's eye, crawling embers in raw flesh—the cadaver standing in the street, transfixed by the caution light.

A strange thought came to him, one that didn't seem quite his own. *Have you seen the yellow sign?* He focused on his progress along the plane of the sidewalk.

As they neared Saul's little house, Malcolm saw his outline standing on the enclosed front porch, the light of a cigarette gently pulsing, another yellow sign. It beckoned them closer, and as Jean and Malcolm went up the walk, the screen door suddenly banged open. The cigarette dropped from Saul's lips.

"Malcolm," he said.

Jean clapped his hands in exultation. "You see him? You see him! He's really there! Saul, he came to me!"

"Get in here," Saul said, and held the door for Jean. He stared directly at Malcolm as the ghost approached, and he wondered exactly what Saul did see. A transparent shade with Malcolm's face? Or something else entirely? How he wished he could ask. Maybe Saul knew a way.

Saul continued to hold the door until Malcolm entered the porch, then shut it. The three of them stood there listening to the rain on the roof. Jean prodded Saul. "Where is he?"

"Right beside you."

"Jesus."

Jean made no effort to hide his smile until Saul said, "He's glaring at you."

So Saul could see his face, then. Furthermore, his face, even if he was unaware of it, was expressive. Could he move his phantom lips? He stared at Saul and did the only thing he could do—as he had with his hands, he imagined speaking from his mouth, and thought: *How do you see me?*

Saul smiled gently. "There'll be time for that later. What I want to know is what happened to you."

"He said—" Jean began, then stopped. "Is he telling you? Am I interrupting?"

"Come inside."

Saul led them into his kitchen, opened a cabinet over the fridge and pulled out two small jars. One had a thick, amber-colored fluid. The other was purple and almost looked like cough syrup. Malcolm looked over Saul's shoulder and saw other jars of other colors stacked within.

Jean pointed to the amber jar. "Malcolm, that's Yellow Sign. That's what I gave you," he blurted, as if it were a perfectly normal thing to say.

Saul didn't blink. "Was it homemade?" he asked, as he unscrewed the two jars he'd brought down.

"Yeah. I made it the way I always do." Jean looked around the room. "I couldn't have fucked it up that bad. It's not possible to fuck it up that bad, right?"

"No, that mixture couldn't have harmed him, even if it wasn't correctly proportioned. If that's what you're saying." Saul poured a bit of the purple fluid into a saucer. He swirled the tip of his pinky in the Yellow Sign, then dipped it in the saucer. "Jean."

Jean turned to face him. Saul wiped his pinky across his brow. "This ought to last until sunup. Look around."

Jean's eyes lit upon Malcolm. "Oh my God."

"The sight comes naturally to very few," Saul said as he put the jars away. He turned to Malcolm. "Jean is intuitive, but he lacks natural ability. If he had it, he wouldn't talk about it so much."

Jean's face fell. "We've been through this…"

"I'm just explaining why I had to lens your eye," Saul said. "And maybe giving you a little shit for it."

Malcolm wanted to know exactly what he looked like to them. He thought the question. "His mouth's moving," Jean said.

"He wants to know what we see," Saul told him. "Malcolm, you're wearing the clothes you were wearing last night. You look tired. You're a bit hazy… it's like a double exposure on our plane, but your face is clear. You're doing a good job of keeping your focus." Saul stepped closer, as if he wanted to put his arm around the ghost. "Many spirits never shake off the disorientation. You're doing well. There's nothing to be upset about. No more sadness." For a second, Malcolm almost believed him.

"He's angry. He thought I'd put poison in his drink," Jean said.

"He looks as if he died in his sleep," Saul said. Then, apologetically, "I'm sorry Malcolm, we're speaking of you like you aren't here."

Ray is dead, Malcolm told them.

Jean read his lips this time. "Ray too?" he exclaimed. "I didn't give him anything! See?"

My body—the body I died in—it's alive, somehow. It's not alive, but it is—it's walking around. It's killing people. Three so far that I know of.

"Killing...?" Saul muttered.

"You mean like a zombie?" Jean crossed his arms. "Now, I've never heard of *that.*"

Saul shushed him and leaned against the counter, chin in hand. "Go on," he told Malcolm.

When all had been told, Jean said, "I can't believe any of this." He pulled a chair away from the little table across from the counter. Slumped there, he looked at Malcolm. "Listen... I was trying to help, like I said. Because I *did* fuck up. But not last night. I gave Leo a reading—"

"Now might not be the time," Saul said.

Jean shook his head. "I told Leo someone new was coming into his life. I didn't say the guy was going to take your place, Malcolm. I didn't tell Leo it was over between the two of you. Just that there was going to be someone new. It was a lie when I said it!"

"Jean." Saul pointed to the doorway. "Go make yourself a drink."

Malcolm glared at Jean as he slunk out of the room. Saul sighed. "One has nothing to do with the other. Now, it isn't uncommon for the spirit and body to become separated by some psychic trauma, and it sounds as if you and your body may still be tethered to one another, which isn't uncommon either. As far as what your body has done—I have to admit, I've never heard of anything like what you've described. However, I'm sure we can complete the separation." Turning, he started taking jars from the cabinet again. He held out the Yellow Sign and said, "Truth." Setting down the purple jar, he said, "Spirit." Besides that, he placed a jar of crimson-tinged ichor. "Nature."

He rifled through a drawer at his waist. "We need to find your body. We have you, so it won't be too difficult. I only hope we get to it before further harm is done."

Jean was in the doorway, drink in hand. "Malcolm."

"Not now," Saul said brusquely.

Jean stared at him, at the jars on the counter. His eyelids fluttered. "Is that—is that Red Death?" He pointed at the crimson jar. "What are you doing with *that?*"

Glass fell somewhere in the rear of the house.

Saul spun around, knocking the purple jar from the counter. His hand shot out to catch it. *"Quiet!"* he hissed, and Jean's half-opened mouth snapped shut.

Jean turned in the doorway, then turned back, his eyes like saucers. The three of them listened. Malcolm tried to seek out the smaller sounds in the house, searching for footfalls on carpet, but all he could hear was the rain and the breathing of the other two.

The lights went out.

Jean screamed. His shadow bolted across the kitchen, toward the front. Saul caught him, and Malcolm heard the muffled sounds of their wrestling, heard Saul whispering, *"The fuse box is that way! We can't go that way!"*

They all knew it was the cadaver.

Saul pulled Jean back toward the next room, and the floor creaked—the sound was answered by another from the front hall. The cadaver had entered from the back and slipped down the hallway. It hadn't barreled mindlessly into the kitchen, it had taken out the lights. It was stalking them.

Malcolm scanned the darkness. *The thing couldn't have followed me to Jean's, waited, and then followed us here, could it?* Malcolm's being was chilled by the realization that the body wasn't merely a rogue vessel, but was possessed of its own intellect. It had been stripped of his mind, had shed his flesh, and was becoming something else— joining some other order between life and death.

Then he saw it,—standing there in the doorway leading from the front hall, the glowing brand on its forehead.

Jean and Saul didn't react. Couldn't they see it? Malcolm stared through the shadows into their vacant eyes. They couldn't see a goddamn thing! *It's there! IT'S RIGHT THERE!*

With a sound like thunder, the cadaver charged into the room.

It ran full-force into Saul. He crashed into Jean, and they went down in a pile, the cadaver spilling over the two men. Screams erupted. All Malcolm could see now was a flurry of thrashing black limbs, and he was panicking—light bloomed at the edges of his spectral vision, and the sounds of the struggle assaulted his sense of orientation. He had begun to think of himself as a person again, standing and talking there in the kitchen. He was suddenly and keenly aware of his formlessness as the screams of Jean and Saul grew distant. *Still yourself. Focus!*

Malcolm hovered over the cadaver's back. He imagined his hands, raised over the thing in balled fists, and saw ectoplasm forming in the air. The noise in the room sharpened: shoes squeaking across linoleum, snapping teeth. *"GET HIM OFF!"* Jean wailed. Saul had to be getting the worst of it. And he wasn't making any sound at all.

Malcolm brought his fists down between the cadaver's shoulder blades. He vaguely felt the contact—numbness on numbness—but the cadaver shot bolt upright and turned its fiery third eye to face him.

It was looking right through him. That didn't matter, because Saul and Jean were wriggling out from under the thing and clawing their way into the next room.

Malcolm reached for the cadaver's face, its raw bleeding flesh puckered and wrinkled like that of an old man. He brushed his fingertips across the bridge of its nose. The thing grunted. *I'm here. Look for me.*

It grunted again, and one dark claw swept through the space where Saul had been. The cadaver whirled and was on its feet. From the darkness beyond, Saul cried, "Jean! Come here, Jean!"

The cadaver lurched forward, and as soon as Malcolm heard Jean's strangled gasp, he could see a silhouette there and knew the thing had him.

Saul's shadow leapt into the fray. Jean was pushed back, and the cadaver caught hold of the older man, then threw him back into the other room, grabbing Jean once more.

Footsteps thumping on carpet. Saul, coming around through the hall...? The footsteps entered the kitchen opposite Jean and the cadaver. Malcolm saw Saul at the counter. He was going after the jars. *Of course!* But then he was gone, and Malcolm heard the front door striking the wall as it flew open, and the porch door clattered noisily seconds later. Saul had fled.

Light swam around Malcolm as he looked back at Jean. He heard meat tearing, Jean gurgling. The cadaver let out a low moan as it buried its face in Jean's body.

When his senses returned, he wasn't sure at first. Though he could again see the details of the kitchen, it was startlingly bright.

Then he saw what was left of Jean.

It had been a feast. As with the policewoman, his flesh had been peeled away in strips. Red lines welled in vertical patterns on the thin layer of meat still clinging to Jean's bones. The cadaver had gorged itself. In the blood covering the floor, Malcolm saw the impression where the thing had sat cross-legged, like a child, beside Jean's corpse. He saw the footprints marking its exit.

It's morning. Jean is dead. Saul is gone. I'm alone.

He never would have expected Saul to flee, he had seen things most people didn't believe in. Malcolm recalled the cadaver hurling Saul away to get at Jean. Lucky.

Or...

He was still "tethered" in some way to the cadaver, and he had been angry at Jean. He'd blamed him for what happened last night, and even though it wasn't true, he now knew that Jean's psychic bullshit had helped Leo justify his affair. It was as if the cadaver had known, and had felt the same rage.

If he and the cadaver were connected that intimately, what then of the attack on the police officers? Malcolm hadn't had anything to do with that. They'd simply been in the wrong place at the wrong time. The thing was driven to feed, that was all, whether or not he gave it direction. But now he was sure he had focused it on Jean. *I'm so sorry. You were trying to help.*

He thought about Ray. That could only have been grim circumstance. Yes, he'd been upset at Ray for being preoccupied with Bonnie, but—

Bonnie.

She was going to Malcolm's this morning. Maybe right now.

The clock on the microwave read 9:30. He still had time. He didn't know what he was going to do. *She is going to see it.* She would see the blood in the hall, and she was a police detective. When neither Malcolm nor Ray responded to her pounding she would kick the door in. *I have to be there.* He had to explain it to her, somehow, before her colleagues ran the bloody fingerprints or—worse yet— found the cadaver.

Then he thought of something else: *What if it's gone after Leo?*

Jesus. Jesus. He willed himself to stay focused. *If that's true… go to Bonnie. Get Bonnie. Get the police.* A few bullets may not have been able to stop the thing, but it was still flesh and blood. It had to have a breaking point.

As he exited the kitchen, he noticed the jars on the counter. Only the Red Death was missing.

The sky was still bloated and gray, and a light drizzle fell as he moved down the street. The gutters were overflowing. It had been one hell of a downpour.

He saw police on Westmore. They surrounded the mouth of the alley where the patrol officers had been killed. He went to the other side of the street. If they were there, it was only a matter of time before they found the scene around the corner, assuming 911 hadn't already been called hours ago. *God, maybe Bonnie's already here, on the job.* He hastened his progress, crossing the street again as he passed the crime scene. He wondered what they were making of it, two cops lying half-devoured in broad daylight.

To think he was seeking out a detective now, after a night of the walking dead and would-be psychics. He had accepted this new reality so easily. He supposed there was no alternative, except maybe to go mad—if the dead were capable of such things—and he suspected he was. Maybe he was mad already, having gone to Jean and Saul first, but he'd had his reasons. It had made sense in the new world.

There were no police around his building. It was Saturday morning—maybe none of his neighbors had left their apartments yet, hadn't seen the mess. That gave him a little time to prepare for Bonnie, and figure out just how he was going to get through to her. With a feeling of hope, he went up the steps and through the entrance.

His door was open, but he'd left it that way. Malcolm passed over dried copper stains and stopped in the doorway.

She was there. She was standing over Ray, hands on her face, her mouth stretched open in s silent scream. Tears streaked the collar of her jacket. She'd been there a while.

The memory of finding his brother, undiminished, unfiltered, came back all at once. Malcolm trembled in space. He searched the room. There was nothing to write in, or with, except... and he refused, absolutely refused. Then he thought again of Leo. He had to get Bonnie over there now.

Malcolm moved to the couch. He cast himself downward, beside Ray. He didn't look at him. He concentrated on the blood that covered everything. He concentrated on the thought of a finger dipping into a dark pool.

She must not have noticed at first, the first vertical line being traced on Ray's forearm. Then the line took a sharp turn. Bonnie's breath caught in her throat. She stumbled back, shaking the tears from her eyes. Another character was printed beside the first. Then another.

L E O

"R-Ray?"

Malcolm looked up in surprise. Bonnie wrung her hands and stepped closer, and repeated, "Ray?"

Just as well she thought that. Maybe it would bring her some small measure of comfort. Jean had been right about one thing— Bonnie loved Ray.

"Leo. What do you mean, Leo? Ray?"

There wasn't time now to explain further. Malcolm printed the name again, this time on Ray's cheek. His digits made gentle impressions in the pale skin. For the first time, he noticed that Ray's hair was going gray on the sides. Even if he could have wept, it would have done nothing. He wanted to tear himself in half.

"Leo? Where is he?" Bonnie pulled her gun from her jacket. Malcolm saw the transformation occur, saw her emotions retreating as she raised the weapon and edged toward the kitchenette. "Is anyone here? Come out!" She glanced over the counter and, seeing nothing, moved toward the bedroom door.

She nudged it open with the back of her hand. "Malcolm?" He heard her sigh—she must have been relieved to find the room empty. She turned back. "Ray? Where's Malcolm? Is he with Leo?" She went back to the body. "I'm going to Leo's. Is that right? Can you tell me? Are you still here?"

Malcolm silently urged her from the hall outside. Finally she came. She moved with purpose, and he had to cast himself out quickly to keep up with her. Leaving the building, she pulled out her phone. He heard her calling in the address and some other numbers, numbers that meant Ray had been ripped apart, as she got into her car by the curb.

Shit! He couldn't ride with her. Malcolm had to get to Leo's on foot, or whatever he had. He looked through the windshield at Bonnie, saw her pulling the runny mascara from her face with her fingers, dropping the gun in the passenger seat. Then she started the car and tore out of the gutter, sending a sheet of rainwater through Malcolm.

He moved after her at a runner's pace, but he felt like he was slogging through mud. Maybe he was relying too much on his orientation on the physical plane, maybe he could travel at the speed of thought if he only knew how, but he didn't. So he chased Bonnie's car and when it accelerated from sight, he followed the streets he used to walk when he was alive.

He saw Bonnie's car, parked and empty, and slowed as he approached the entrance to Leo's building. It had been weeks since he'd seen Leo, heard his voice, or even read his words. And Leo would never see him again. So, then. No awkward overtures, not even a last shouting match. The matter was finished. Malcolm didn't know how to feel about that. He wasn't sure that the living could have arranged a more satisfying resolution.

He went in. Leo's place was on the first floor, last door on the right. It was closed. Malcolm passed through.

Same old place. Same magazines piled on the couch cushion nearest the door, same big blue candle sitting unlit on the kitchen counter. He tried to imagine that familiar old smell and found he couldn't.

Voices from the back. Malcolm went down the hall.

Bonnie was in Leo's room. She was in his face, screaming as he stood against a half-tilted desk chair, as if he'd been roused from work by her screaming. "What happened? *TELL ME!*"

"I don't know what you're talking about! Calm the hell down!"

"He told me!" Bonnie's voice was ragged. She was crying again. "He *told* me! Now you can be a friend, and talk to me, or I can take you in and you can fucking talk to them!"

She grabbed Leo's wrist. He jerked away. His ankle caught the leg of the chair and he fell against the wall. Pages from a wall calendar tore away under his shoulder. "Bonnie! I can't talk to you until you talk to me! What happened to Ray? Is Malcolm all right?"

"I don't know where Malcolm is," she snapped. "Maybe you do."

Malcolm was almost between them now, trying to think of something, anything, to let them know: *I'm here!*

"I don't know *anything!*" He wormed along the wall as she grabbed handfuls of his sweater. "You're crazy," he breathed.

"What?" She reached into her jacket. Leo tried to shove past her. She knocked him back, into the window blinds, with a crash. His face flushed, and his hand closed into a fist. For a second, Bonnie's eyes widened.

The cadaver's arms plowed through the blinds with a shriek of glass, wrapping around Leo's chest, jerking him back into—*through*—the window. Glass crunched and spilled onto the carpet as the blinds were warped out of shape. The dead man's head pushed through, blood dribbling from its lipless mouth. Bonnie stood frozen as she watched Leo being pulled out in a tangle of vinyl and flesh.

Light and sound surrounded Malcolm, and he lost sight of Leo's sneakers as they kicked in the air. He felt like he was being swept away by a funeral dirge. Vaguely, he picked out the front door banging open. Voices, again, this time Bonnie and someone else.

Saul!

Malcolm focused in and saw the man cradling Bonnie, turning her away from the window. "It took him?" Saul barked. "It took him? Alive?"

"I don't know!" Bonnie sobbed.

"It's all right." He held her against his chest.

"How did you know?" Her sobbing was muffled now. Malcolm stared into Saul's eyes, and Saul stared back.

"I followed him," Saul said. "He killed Jean last night. And Ray."

"Was it…"

"It was Malcolm," Saul said, still looking at the ghost.

What are you doing? Malcolm cried.

"Malcolm? It looked like him. A little. But why?"

"It would be best if I took it from here," Saul said. His gaze held nothing but contempt. It seemed to say to Malcolm, *Why do you still believe in people?*

Malcolm, it seemed, had overlooked the obvious yet again.

He watched without feeling as his murderer ushered Bonnie from the room. "I'm going with you," she was saying. "Whatever's going on, whatever you're going to do, I'm going with you. Ray spoke to me."

She sounded just like poor Jean—so hopeful, so excited to finally have had a haunting of her very own. As if there were really any answers, any comfort in the knowledge of spirits. It only meant that miserable existence didn't end with death.

Malcolm cast himself after them. Saul was glancing over his shoulder as he took Bonnie to the front door. "We should go alone," he said, eyes fixed on Malcolm. "Very bad things could happen if we didn't."

Malcolm stopped. *Who is he threatening? Is he going to hurt her? Leo, his lover?*

"Good," Saul said, and he and Bonnie left.

Who had Saul followed—Malcolm or the cadaver? He'd shadowed the ghost, most likely; would have been far safer, and both inevitably ended up in the same place anyway. Malcolm had taken the thing off autopilot again when he returned to consciousness that morning, and had led it to Leo, bringing his worst fears to fruition. Only now it was so much worse.

He turned from the front door and went back to the bedroom window. There was a small lawn in the back of the building. Beyond a chain-link fence, the lawn sloped downward into what looked like a drainage ditch. Beyond that, a dense spread of trees. Malcolm passed through the wall and went to the fence. The ditch had a small river of rainwater in it, flowing into a large concrete pipe with an iron grate. There were holes in the fence. The cadaver could have gone down there to feed.

Malcolm went through the fence and to the edge of the water. No sign of the cadaver or Leo. Again he looked at the big pipe. From this angle he could see that the iron grate was actually partially loose, pried away from the opening. He moved into the water, for just a second he expected to splash down and encounter icy resistance. There was none, and he cast himself forth. The rushing water caught the ectoplasm, and he was wrenched violently forward. *Jesus!* The ectoplasm broke apart, and he was in the middle of the ditch, barely atop the water. *Okay. Careful now. Don't cast too far.* He didn't want to be sucked right past them, if they were in the pipe.

Into the darkness. Sound cascading off the concrete walls. Malcolm focused himself forward. He didn't see them, not yet. He wondered what Saul's intentions were. It didn't seem like he could track the cadaver without the ghost's help.

Unless he can track Leo.

Who knew what Saul was capable of? All those weird jars of color in his kitchen. Yellow Sign, Red Death. He'd taken the Red Death with him. *Why? Did I ever known the real Saul?* It didn't seem that the mentor he'd yearned for was ever there. Not for him, anyway. For Leo, yes.

Don't think about Leo. Don't get angry. He saw light streaming into the tunnel from fissures in the ceiling, through which dangled soggy strands of blanched grass. The morning light struck through a brownish haze in the tunnel, and Malcolm became aware of how dark the water was down here. Tendrils of other fluids snaked along the surface, oily, foul-looking stuff. It swam around the edges of a concrete partition that looked half-finished. Lengths of rebar jutted out from it, and Malcolm saw something caught on one of them. It was a ragged thing, like snakeskin, blood gleaming on its surface. It was cadaver-skin.

Malcolm passed through the partition and into a new tunnel, this one stained and splattered with waste. He realized where he was. This was part of the defunct storm-water system that led to Old Valley Municipal. There was evidence of the private developer's half-hearted attempts to seal it off, but sure enough, it was the new system that had led Malcolm here. Ray wouldn't have had any trouble winning this one. The water was black with whatever the developer was dumping. Another tunnel branched off from it, sloping upward toward the surface. Malcolm ascended it, as he assumed the cadaver had, and emerged from a hole in the middle of the woods.

The drizzle had subsided, though the sky was still suffused with gray. He saw the remnants of the old treatment plant through the trees. He heard a distant that may have been the cry of a bird, or a man. *Leo's alive. It wants him, just like I did.*

Brown pools dotted the ground surrounding the plant. Above-ground tanks and pumping stations, threaded with dense pipe-works and unhealthy-looking vines, rose from the spoiled earth. Malcolm listened intently. He heard another cry, and saw a large black bird sitting atop one of the tanks. It looked directly at him and shrieked. When he drew closer, it lit into the air and was gone.

A metal door in the side of the tank lay open. Malcolm entered into its shadows. Water dripping noisily from the ceiling inside. He could make out a steel walkway, going over a pool that must have been used to remove sediment. It was half-full of gray water gone black.

Malcolm crossed the walkway. A door on the opposite side led into a narrow stairwell, which led him below ground again. He entered an unlit corridor, he was barely able to make out any detail from the light trickling down the stairs. Unable to feel the floor or walls, he almost felt lost in a limitless void—until he heard Saul's voice bouncing down the hall.

A flashlight's beam cut through the darkness some yards away. Malcolm moved to the wall, slipping partway into its steel-and-earth structure to conceal himself, as Saul and Bonnie searched the corridor. Bonnie tried a door while Saul consulted a control box in the opposite wall. A second later, buzzing lights flickered to life on the ceiling.

Bonnie jiggled the handle on the door. "Look at the floor." She pointed out a set of damp prints with her gun. "They went in here." She brought the butt of the gun down on the handle and wrenched the door open with a groan. "Down again."

"Let me go first."

"Saul, what the hell is going on?"

"Malcolm…" Saul cocked his head. He glanced subtly to a side, and he saw the ghost.

"He is beyond help, that's all I know." He stepped back, allowing Bonnie to take point. When she went through the door, Saul turned to Malcolm, and the ghost swept into his face. Saul showed no fear. "I lied. I can help you, and I will. You'll be at pace."

WHAT DID YOU DO?

"It wasn't my fault," Saul sighed. "I knew Jean was going to slip you Yellow Sign at the Arms. I didn't need any spirit guides to tell me, it was his nature. He didn't know about Leo and I. Poor Jean, always wanting to be involved.

"So I brought a little Red Death. I put it in your drink before he added the Sign. It tastes sweet, and goes down like silk. It doesn't feel like what it is. I gave you just the right amount, but he must have used too little Sign for them to fuse properly."

WHAT DID YOU DO? Malcolm's senses were wavering. Saul knew it, too, his calm was causing Malcolm to come unhinged all the quicker.

"Yellow Sign clears and focuses the third eye. Red Death corrodes it. A cocktail unknown to western doctors and detectives alike. You should have been drawn out completely when their combined effects overtook you, but you're still tethered to the cadaver, snagged on some bit of temporal filth on that lens.

"I can't pull you free now. And it obviously can't pull you back in. I think the poor thing's just an empty vessel seeking substance. Nature abhors a vacuum, we remember." Reaching into the pockets of his coat, he produced a pair of hypodermic syringes, each filled with what could only be Red Death. "Two more doses ought to kill the brain for good."

What will happen to me?

"Truthfully, I don't know," Saul said. "And, really, I don't care."

Malcolm had only his words at this point, he could no more stand in Saul's path than he could knock the son of a bitch out. So he spoke. *He still loves me. That's why you did it.*

Saul laughed, but the laugh was a lie.

Maybe he never loved you, Saul. Maybe it was all magic and potions.

"No!"

Then it was manipulation. You've made it your life's work. You're a monster.

"I'll kill you!" Saul screamed.

Bonnie called his name from the darkness. He stiffened. "I'll kill *him*," he snarled. "And her. I swear it."

Then it was Bonnie who screamed.

Saul's threats vanished as his eyes widened and he whispered, "Leo!"

He raced through the door. Malcolm tore after him, through a waste-splattered passage that sloped and twisted downward, beneath lights that flickered and popped excitedly. Saul slipped and crashed against the wall. Malcolm shot past him, casting himself forward as quickly as he could. *Leo!*

The sloping floor became level again after the next turn. There, Bonnie was in the grip of the cadaver. Leo was nowhere to be seen. The corpse's hands were wrapped around Bonnie's throat, and her gun lay on the floor below her dangling feet. Clawing at the cadaver's raw cheeks, pulling away strings of flesh, she gurgled Malcolm's name. Like Ray, she believed it was him. She wouldn't know otherwise until she was already dead, and maybe not even then.

Leo emerged from an alcove behind the cadaver with a rusty pipe in his hands, and he brought it down on the cadaver's neck with all his strength. The thing buckled over, dropping Bonnie. As she hit the floor, her foot kicked the gun away.

Saul rounded the corner. "Get away from it!"

The cadaver turned to Leo, who hit it across the face with the pipe, sending shards of teeth flying from its mouth as it fell back.

"Leo, get back!" Saul cried.

Malcolm looked from Saul to the cadaver, then back. And *focused*.

The cadaver straightened up. Leo stood between it and Bonnie, ready to strike again, but the thing turned to Saul.

"No," the old man breathed. "Malcolm, stop it. Don't—you don't have it in you—"

Leo snatched up Bonnie's gun, but she grabbed his arm and tugged him back. "No!" he said. "We can't leave him!"

"Give me the gun!" Bonnie's shout reverberated through Malcolm as he watched the scene unfold.

Leo handed the pistol over, and Bonnie tried to find a shot, but the cadaver was already upon Saul, seizing his head in both hands and lifting him off the floor. Saul's eyes fluttered in his face.

The cadaver released him.

At first Malcolm thought Saul had used some sort of secret command, but then the thing turned, and he saw the needle protruding from its chest just below the collarbone. The syringe was empty. The cadaver staggered, fell against the wall. Then the entire world began to transform—Malcolm's world, his perception—color draining away and sound fading. The poison was affecting him too. He fought to steady himself while the cadaver stumbled past him.

It was after Bonnie and Leo again. They fled down the hall, deeper into the plant. Saul sat on the floor and held his head. "Almost...killed me. Malcolm..."

He looked at the ghost. Saul was black-and-white now, his edges soft and indistinct. Malcolm's point of view yawed from side to side. Saul rose—he looked more confident than ever—and pulled the other syringe from his coat. "One more, Malcolm. Then it's over. You're over."

His voice went in out, and then the thrumming chaos of the world around Malcolm—the spitting and crackling of the lights, the howls of the empty pipe-works, the distant pleas of the cadaver's prey—overwhelmed him. He couldn't see anymore. He felt Saul passing through him, heard the man mutter something. Malcolm fought to regain his foothold in the corporeal, he tried to clear his mind of panic over what would happen to Leo if the cadaver were left to its own devices, and over what might happen to him if Saul landed that second needle in its back. One way or another, he didn't believe he was long for the world. He had to make sure he went out alone.

The world resolved into a gray blur. He was able to make out the details of the corridor, and began moving sluggishly after the others.

The corridor opened into a huge concrete vault. The others were on a grated platform overlooking a pool of waste. Bonnie and Leo coughed violently as they crowded against the railing. The fumes must have been terrible, but they were cornered by the cadaver and there was no other way out but the way they'd come. It stood uncertainly before them. Bonnie raised the gun. *"Saul, move!"*

He was weaving back and forth behind the cadaver. Still stunned from the earlier attack, Saul was fighting to stay on his feet. He held out the syringe and yelled, *"I have him! Here is his last moment!"*

The cadaver lunged at Bonnie. The gun went off in its face. It spun away, its cheekbone sheared away, embers spewing from the sign in its forehead, then snapped back, grabbing hold of her hair. She threw her arms out. Leo was knocked off-balance, and Malcolm saw the railing giving way under his weight, watched as Leo went over.

Saul and Malcolm reached the railing just in time to see Leo splash down. He came up immediately, but only half his head and his thrashing hands were visible. "Get out of there! Get to the ledge!" Saul pointed frantically to a slab of concrete jutting from the wall on Leo's left.

Leo coughed, then screamed—in pain. "I can't!"

"What do you mean?" Saul cried.

Malcolm looked to the cadaver and Bonnie. For a second, he had forgotten all about her, the last friend he had left. Both of the cadaver's hands were tangled in her hair, and it beat on her back as it tried to fit its broken jaw upon the crown of her head.

Malcolm turned back to Saul. He was paying no attention to Bonnie's struggle. "The ledge!" he shouted.

"I can't!" Leo repeated, shaking his head in the muck. "My leg!"

Has to be either broken or caught in something—Malcolm focused—*I'll cast myself down to the water*—

There was a sickening snap from the end of the platform. The cadaver had Bonnie's hand folded back against her arm. Her mouth was open in a silent scream. With its other hand, still in her hair, it smashed her head against the railing, its gaze fixed upon Saul before she hit the floor.

Saul held out the syringe. "Come on, then."

Blood pulsed from Bonnie's temple and dripped through the grating, down to where Leo struggled and screamed. Very little time left, one way or the other. Once either Saul or the cadaver was dead, there would be no time.

Malcolm moved in front of him. *Leo's stuck. I'll try to get him free. Just wait.*

"He's not yours to save," Saul growled.

Only I can get down there! Only you can hold off the cadaver! Think!

Saul shook his head.

If you love him, Malcolm said, and then cast himself down.

The falling ectoplasm penetrated the jelly-like scum on the surface of the pool. As Malcolm went under, his vision went from black-and-white to sepia. He found himself fixed just beneath the surface, a few feet from the flailing Leo, whose head was barely above water. As Leo's arms churned the water, light struck through, and Malcolm was able to see the junk lying at the bottom of the vault—warped steel barrels, chunks of concrete, and rebar spears pointed toward the surface. Leo's right ankle had been skewered on one, a black cloud hung around his trembling leg.

Malcolm cast ectoplasm toward the bottom. It broke up almost immediately, and he barely moved. He cast again, and again. Inch by inch he drew closer to Leo. He didn't know how he was going to be able to concentrate his imagined fingers around Leo's ankle, worse yet, he didn't know if he'd even make it down there. His vision was flashing now. Saul might already have planted the second syringe in the cadaver's heart. Maybe he'd rather let Leo drown than allow Malcolm to save him, even if Leo himself wouldn't know it was him.

That strengthened his resolve, and he struck downward with unbroken concentration until he was right beside Leo's speared leg. He imagined hands around the ankle. He was going to need the leverage of arms to do this, too, and so he willed them to be. He felt resistance as ectoplasm formed around fingers and wrists, bringing them into the corporeal, then the ectoplasm fragmented, and he was limbless once more. *Goddammit!*

Can't do it. Can barely see a thing. Slipping…fading…have to stop thinking like a person. Think like a ghost. Ghosts don't have hands, or arms, you're just imagining them where you'd expect them to be.

That was it. He cast himself upward, passed through the surface into the air. Leo was sputtering, trying to force black slime from his mouth, tiring. On the platform above, Saul danced around the lumbering cadaver. *"Malcolm!"* he bellowed.

Fixed just above the surface, Malcolm focused without sight on Leo's foot. He imagined his hands, still beneath the water, still down at the bottom, coalescing around it. Gripping it, if only for a second, before the ectoplasm eroded. And at the same time he cast himself upward as far as he could.

His perspective shifted violently as ectoplasm went up into the air, then rained down. He was pulled into the slime again. But he'd felt it, on the upstroke—he'd pulled Leo's foot maybe an inch.

Leo screamed in agony. Malcolm ignored it and imagined his hands. He felt Leo's shoe and cast upward again.

I don't need to be underwater, sluggish and weak, to pull Leo. I can do it from up here. At least above he had a bit more power, so he cast himself upward again, and again, and when Leo's foot came free he felt it, and Leo immediately kicked toward the ledge. He slung his arms over it and coughed violently. His breathing sounded terrible.

Malcolm remembered there were fumes there that he couldn't inhale. He focused his hands beneath Leo's arms and hoisted him up in one final cast, onto the ledge, then hovered over the pool. He looked to Saul, who had seen Leo, and was now moving in for the kill. He looked back at Leo one last time.

Leo's head was lying against the concrete, facing away from him, but Malcolm heard him say, "Thank you, thank you." He had never believed in God…he must have learned to believe in something.

Malcolm was hit by a wave of disorientation that seemed to spin the world around him. He tried to cast as light bloomed, and he couldn't. There was nowhere to cast. There was nothing to cast.

There was nothing.

"I'll get you up," Saul called hoarsely to Leo. "Hold on."

Bonnie stirred. She gripped her broken wrist and let out a sharp wail. Saul went to her. "I need your help. Do you have a phone?" He reached into her jacket.

"What…" She lifted her head and saw the cadaver lying on its back, the second syringe in its shoulder.

"We need to call for help," Saul told her. "I can barely breathe. Leo must be suffocating down there."

Bonnie was still looking at the cadaver, and the syringe. "What is that?"

"Poison. It's dead."

"How did you know to do that?"

"A magician never reveals his secrets," Saul said, forcing a smile, and offered Bonnie his hand.

A raw, skeletal claw fell upon his shoulder. It tightened until he shrieked in pain, hauling him to his feet. The cadaver hurled him across the platform. Saul bounced off the far wall and crumpled to the floor. "Help me!" he gasped.

The cadaver looked down at Bonnie. It plucked the syringe from its shoulder, its shattered jaw moved, and she heard a faint moan, as if it were trying to form words.

It knelt and touched its fingers to her temple. She sat rigid, looking only into its eyes, until it touched those same fingers to her leg. In her blood, in that same blocky handwriting, it printed: $MALCOLM$

She understood, and accepted it.

"What happened to you?" she whispered through tears.

The cadaver turned from her without answering. It went to Saul.

He wanted so badly to explain. He wanted to explain it all, before he went away, he wanted his proper ending. But, in truth, he still didn't understand it all himself. He didn't know how he was back in his body, or how he was able to move through such unimaginable pain. But he was, and he collected Saul and drew him into an embrace. He turned toward the railing. Saul screamed a litany of curses, some profane, others in tongues Malcolm didn't recognize. The old man beat his head against Malcolm's skull, and the last embers of the yellow sign fell away.

They stood at the edge of the platform, Malcolm gripping Saul in a crushing bear hug, staring into his face until their eyes met.

This will have to do for an ending.

He leaned forward, and they tumbled into the pool.

The rebar pierced them both. Saul's last scream bubbled from his throat, followed by a dark mist. They floated in silence on the skewers. Then, it was just Malcolm.

Then no one.

I love you Leo, and Bonnie, and Ray. I love you, Jean. It's all I am now. This beautiful light.

Forevermore.

About the Authors

Orpheus & The Pearl Author
Kim Paffenroth

Dr. Kim Paffenroth is a professor of religious studies at Iona College, and the author of several books on the Bible and theology. He grew up in New York, Virginia, and New Mexico. He attended St. John's College, Annapolis, MD (BA, 1988), Harvard Divinity School (MTS, 1990), and the University of Notre Dame (PhD, 1995). He now lives in upstate New York with his wife and two kids.

His work in the horror genre includes *Gospel of the Living Dead: George Romero's Visions of Hell on Earth* (Baylor, 2006) - Winner, 2006 Bram Stoker Award; *Dying to Live: A Novel of Life among the Undead* (Permuted Press, 2007); and *Dying to Live: Life Sentence* (Permuted Press, 2008). His newest is *Valley of the Dead* (Permuted Press, 2010). He has also edited the anthologies *History Is Dead* (Permuted Press, 2007), and *The World Is Dead* (Permuted Press, 2009).

Nevermore, or The Feast of Flesh Author
David Dunwoody

David Dunwoody is the author of the zombie novel *Empire*, as well as the horror collections *Dark Entities* and *Unbound & Other Tales*. Dave lives in Utah and can be visited on the web at daviddunwoody. com.